The Shadow Dies Loudly

The Shadow Dies Loudly

27 Tales

T.L Oberheu

Boxhead Books

CONTENTS

1

Acknowledgements

Words cannot describe how grateful I am that you picked up this book. Within these pages are several years worth of stories and my evolution as a writer. My first book *Twist and Shout: An Awkward Life With Tourette's* was my first attempt at getting officially published, and without saying how that did, I was told to "stick to fiction".

So I did.

The stories in this collection span quite some time. The first one in the collection was written in 2014, and it was actually the first short story I wrote in a college setting. But the 26th story was based off of a story I wrote in 3rd grade, which says a lot about how I was as a child when you think about.

Anyway, here I'd like to thank all the people that made this book possible. First off I'd like to thank my dear friends John Paul, Nicole Rhim, Jake Malinowski, and my father Larry Oberheu for reading these stories when they were just a collection of google docs. I'd also like to thank those four again, as well as Julia Paul, Carl Michaelson, Declan Walker, Juliet Polaski, "B" (my good friend from Virginia with the amazing podcast *Arbitrary Advice)* my family in Curtice, Ohio, and many more who wish to remain anonymous, for voting in the poll I created to choose the amazing cover of this book.

Of course, I also have to shout out my cover artist, and plug her website where she does amazing designs:

http://www.cakamuradesigns.com/

And of course an tremendous thank you to my incredible editor Taylor J. Hale, whose an amazing author as well. Ms. Hale made this book the way it is since my grammatical skills are that of a five year old, as well as gave some great advice on turning these stories from college classroom tier to a published book tier.

Thank you all for helping me on this journey!

2

The Beast He Was

It was midnight when the two men in the subway car were figuring out how they were going to kill each other. The older man took a long drink from his worn silver flask and never broke eye contact with the younger.

"You know why I'm here," said the older man.

"I have no idea what you're talking about," said the younger man through a disturbingly large grin.

The older took another drink. He slouched in his seat casually—he'd done this before. "You recognized me the minute I sat down. It wasn't that hard to find you, you know? I figured you'd be here."

"How so?"

"Because this is the only subway that you haven't killed anyone on."

A pause hung in the air, each man studying the other.

"Once again, old man, I haven't the faintest clue what you're talking about."

The younger man tried to hold back from smiling so much, but how can you not smile when you're having so much fun?

"Subtlety is not a gift that you have is it?" asked the older man.

Noticing the older man's badge, the younger man spoke up, "Officer...."

"Detective," the old man interjected.

"Detective, you should probably put down the flask and stop saying such strange things. You'll scare the other passengers."

The detective looked around the empty train, wondering if this man was just a smart ass or truly insane.

He took another drink.

"Cut the shit, you obviously know who I am, and I know who you are, so just spare me the games and let's talk", the older man demanded.

"Now, what would you like to discuss sir?"

"You."

"Well, I'm just flattered, but not interested." The younger man giggled. The call to paint the car with the older man's insides grew stronger.

"Let's get one thing straight: I am going to put you down like the beast you are."

"That's not very police-like of you, don't I get a trial? Read my Miranda Rights?"

"I know why you killed over two dozen people—I want to hear you say it."

The younger man stared at him for a while, his eyes black and dead. They died a long time ago. The howl of the train and the clicking on the tracks was the only other company he had tonight. He began to realize that this night was only going to end in one of two outcomes. His grin began to shrink.

The younger man ran his tongue over his teeth. "Who's going to miss a few rapists, murderers, and thieves? A little spring cleaning for the city doesn't hurt anyone does it? You of all people should understand. As a matter of fact, I believe a 'thank you' is in order."

Cut from the same fucking cloth, you realize that? No different "

"Of course I'm different! I don't rape or steal from my victims. All I do is cut away at all the filth inside them. I let the blood run out. It's like sin. It flows throughout the subway platform and city streets. Stains clothes. Makes a mess. But while they make it look disgusting in the end, at least they're clean in the only way it really counts."

"What in God's name is wrong with you?"

The younger man glared at the detective, his grin replaced with an animalistic look of rage and hate that came from a past long buried.

"You want to know what's wrong with me? You ever see a loved one get raped? How about murdered? You ever have your dad beat the shit out of you because you spent his drug money on some fucking pizza, because you haven't eaten in a day? You ever live through that, Detective? No, you haven't. You were probably some dumb-shit jock bully whose dad was hard on him because his grades weren't up to par. You probably joined the force right away so you could impress Daddy, or maybe it's just because you weren't smart enough to get into a four-year college. You're an aging, alcoholic bully with a God complex—you'll never understand what's 'wrong' with me."

The detective just sat there. He took another long drink from his flask and held eye contact. He adjusted his trench coat and leaned in. The younger man grimaced from the alcohol emitting from the older man's pores. The older man gazed into his eyes.

"You wanna hear a story, kid?" the older man said, speech slightly slurred. "Ten years ago, there were a few disappearances around a shopping mall in a town I used to live before I got transferred here. It was all young girls, ages fifteen to twenty. After the third disappearance, we had a squad car at that mall every day, all day long. I was in my car, undercover, wouldn't even know who I was while looking at it. At about hour eleven of a very long shift, when I saw her. Pretty, blonde, wearing clothes that her father wouldn't approve of. I watched her walking through the parking lot alone, and when she passed by a row of cars and out of my line of sight, I didn't see her walk out the other end of that row. Just then, a black SUV pulled out of its spot and started driving down the lane. You're damn right I followed."

The detective paused, gaze unwavering.

"He led me to a house a few miles away and pulled into his garage. I was new and scared, and frankly, I was just working on a hunch, but I knew this wrong. I kicked in the door, and when I entered the house, I followed the sounds of muffled screams to the kitchen. The house was dark, the windows had been covered. It looked like nobody had been living there for weeks, or at least—no man. When I got to the kitchen, that girl was hog-tied, bound with jump-rope and gagged with her own sock, missing about a fist-sized chunk of her left thigh. The man stood up from his 'dinner' and stared at me with a mouth full of blood and eyes as dead as a shark's, just like yours. I remember staring into those eyes for what seemed like hours. Two black holes. . He wasn't a man, not anymore. I grabbed him by the neck and threw him down his basement stairs. And then I put him down like the beast he was. I've spent decades putting down beasts. Probably even killed your dead-beat dad. Who knows? I've lost count."

The younger man, almost captivated by the detective, leaned in closer. "Exactly how are you and I any different from one another?"

"We're not. But I have a badge."

They stayed in silence. The howling of the train ringing out like a chorus cheering on the upcoming fight. The detective took another drink and said, “This train has got to stop eventually.”

“And your flask is going to run dry, eventually, Detective. You may be some tough vigilante cop who gets away with murder, but one day, that’s going to stop.”

“Is that so?”

“I guarantee it”.

The conductor spoke over the train intercom: “The final destination is coming up”

It was five a.m. when the group of people were lined in front of the station. The train pulled up, and when the doors opened, some screamed, and one fainted at the sight within the car.

One young man rushed in to see if he could help.

Two men lied in pools of blood, and from the initial looks of it, they were both shot in the neck. The train goers would never forget the sight of carnage that day.

Neither would the conductor as he sat in the front car and put the photos he took with the others.

No one would know he was a warrior who conquered chaos itself.

No one would know he was an artist who put away the personification of the old order.

No one would know the good and the bad he did.

No one would know the beast he was.

3

A Man Walk Into a Bar

Paul smiled as the brunette eyed him from across the bar. Those eyes. Those legs. Jesus Christ, there was no way she was actually into him, right?

Alone at a table, she would coyly glance at him every now and then, only to look away when he noticed. This little game continued for a bit until Paul gathered the strength to go introduce himself. He stumbled when he got off the stool. Shit I hope she didn't see that, Paul thought to himself. He wobbled around the bar to go meet his possible companion for the night.

Thoughts raced through his mind:

I'm fine.

I always get this drunk anyway, and I haven't had a problem yet.

I'm sure I can drive home.

My dick will totally work.

"Hello," said Paul to the girl.

"Hi there," she said with a wink.

"What's your name?" he asked, slurring his speech.

"Claudia".

"That's a nice name." Paul slyly rose a finger to his face. "I see you!"

Clearly, he was nailing this.

"I think you've had enough to drink there, honey."

"No, no, I'm good!"

Claudia gave a coy smile. Her hazel eyes gleaming at the sight of him. "Just checking... I want you to be able to feel everything later tonight." Claudia looked right into Paul's soul. She gave the impression that she was the type of girl who took what she wanted with no questions asked. But there was some pain behind her eyes, just a touch of it. Masked behind her primal hunger, an unspeakable urge for something. An urge for... him?

"We should get out of here, shouldn't we?" she asked.

Paul couldn't be any smoother, any luckier than he was tonight. This sexy little MILF was going to get her world rocked.

The duo walked out of the bar, into the parking lot. The night sky contained no stars.

"I'll drive," slurred Paul.

"Of course," Claudia said. Her laugh was unsettling, but Paul passed it off as him just being too drunk. "But you didn't drive here, sweetie. Remember? You took a taxi."

Paul let out a drunk cackle. "Hey, you're right! But how did you..."

"Because when you killed that little girl while drunk driving, your lawyer daddy got you a deal. You lost your license and spent a few months in prison. He settled the case with the parents, gave them all the money in the world. But there really isn't a price you can put on a child's life, is there?"

Paul frowned in confusion. How could she know that? He didn't have time to think long before a pain struck the back of his head and everything went black.

When Paul woke up, his head was killing him. This wasn't like any hangover he'd ever had before.

Claudia walked over to him with a man. They both wore surgical scrubs and rubber gloves.

"Hello, honey," said Claudia. "How are you feeling?"

Paul started hyperventilating and pissed on the table he was strapped to.

"Oh, are we scared?" said the man. "Our daughter was scared when she was fighting for her life in the hospital. She didn't know if she was going to make it out. But you know she didn't, don't you? You fucking know what you did."

The man started to shake with rage. He punched Paul several times in the face before Claudia stopped him.

"We need him conscious, Kevin."

Tears began to flow down Paul's cheeks before he wept uncontrollably. He opened his mouth to plead and beg and apologize, but Claudia stuffed his own underwear into his mouth. Paul gagged, and bile rose to his throat. But he didn't choke on it. God would not allow that easy of a fate.

Kevin prepared the IV of donor blood. "Blood loss would be too easy of a death for you. Tyra didn't die of blood loss. She didn't have that luxury. She felt so much pain toward the end. I could see it on her angelic face. She knew nothing but pain in her last moments."

They started by breaking his feet. Claudia used a hammer, slamming into the soft flesh. The thud it made as the metal shattered bone brought a smile to Claudia's face. Kevin had more rage in him, so he did it with his bare hands, crunching his toes like glow sticks. Then he clipped off each toe with garden sheers, the spraying his scrubs.

Paul screamed through his gag. The couple wondered if the act of hyperextending his legs caused him to faint or was it merely the deafening pop each one made.

When Paul awoke again, he thought that was just a bad dream. But after looking around the basement where he lay and tasting the skid marks on his underwear, he knew this was far from over.

The vengeful parents went to his arms, breaking each finger at each joint, then his wrists and his elbows. Then they cut off his ears. Claudia waved Paul's own severed ear in front of his face, laughing manically. Kevin took a spoon and dug out Paul's eyes.

The feeling of the blunt tool digging into the eye socket and severing the optic nerve was the worst part so far.

Claudia removed the underwear from Paul's mouth.

He couldn't breathe. He couldn't move anything. He begged to a God that turned away from him long ago.

Kevin picked up the garden sheers. "It's Father's Day today. Did you know that? Too bad you'll never be one."

Paul couldn't see any of this, but he felt the man grab his scrotum and penis. The instrument that did his thinking earlier at that bar laid on the floor, an oozing wound took it's place.

Paul screamed. Claudia held his mouth open as Kevin clipped his tongue and tore each tooth out. Pain wasn't a thing Paul felt anymore, however this done for the message.

"Okay buddy. Let's not ruin the family party. We gotta get going."

The Blanchard family gathered in the living room. Paul wasn't normally late. "Probably drunk again," was the main hypothesis going around. Suddenly, the doorbell rang. The family gathered in silence as they watched Paul squirming on the front porch. Naked, blind, disabled, and disfigured.

"Happy Father's Day. Love, Tyra," was carved into his chest.

4

The Greatest Film Ever Made

Ben was six years old, and he knew nothing.

He was the son of two doctors and the big brother of Mary, who was severely handicapped.

She had been born both deaf and blind. Since she never spoke, her parents assumed she was also mute. Years later, when they would watch The Greatest Film Ever Made, they would learn she could make some noises.

Ben was quite the trouble maker. He had this little habit of ripping the tags off womens' bras whenever his mother took him to the department store. He liked how the breasts looked on the little piece of paper that he would quickly shove into his pockets.

At school, Ben tried to give his female classmates his fruit snacks in exchange for a quick look up their skirts or under their shirts. Nobody caught Ben, however. Even he was surprised that no one ever told on him, so this continued.

Unchecked.

Unbalanced.

Undisciplined.

When Ben was eight years old, he knew a few things.

His older cousin, Dylan, frequently babysat Ben and his sister.

While Dylan looked after the kids, he would watch funny movies on the computer sometimes , but Ben wasn't allowed to join.

One night, Ben creeped downstairs and finally saw the funny movie. He didn't know what was happening, but he liked it.

A man and a lady were naked? How hilarious!

He saw Dylan starring at the screen, smiling, with a blanket over his lap. There was a lot of movement under the blanket. Ben asked Dylan what he was doing.

Dylan jumped and screamed. He looked really scared and said a lot of bad words at Ben, who started to cry.

Dylan told Ben that if he didn't tell anyone, he'd let him watch more funny movies with him. Ben liked the funny movies, so he and Dylan pinkie promised, and Ben never told anyone.

Ben was sixteen years old. He knew a lot.

Dylan was pretty old now, but he wasn't lame like the other adults. He gave Ben his passwords for the various websites he was a member of.

Ben would wake up early, watch some online movies, get ready and go to school, watch some more movies when no one was looking, go home, watch movies, and pass out in a pile of sweat and filth.

A lot of the ladies in the movies seemed really happy. A few didn't. Ben liked when they weren't that happy.

One day, Dylan told Ben about a few secret websites. You had to toy around with your PC, but you could watch all kinds of movies. Some of them were even illegal.

Ben knew that was wrong, but he was curious. He downloaded some stuff, and gained access to some of the most fucked up shit imaginable.

Ben was eighteen years old. He knew everything.

First, he knew about the videos where the lady was tied up.

Then he found out about the ones where the lady would eat a living goldfish or stomp on a small animal.

Then Ben found the rape videos.

Ben knew it was fake, but he wanted more. He hadn't seen Dylan in a long time, and he wouldn't answer his phone.

Ben found out about some incredibly bizarre videos one day.

The lady would die at the end.

Literally. Ben would watch the lady's face turn red as she gasped for air in an erotic mix of pain and suffering, all while the cum would bubble up and out of her bleeding mouth.

Ben watched these videos several times a day.

Then he got bored of those too.

He wanted to make his own.

Mary was twelve years old and knew nothing.

Literally nothing.

Ben knew she cost too much money to have around the house.

He was thinking of his parents when he decided to make The Greatest Film Ever made.

He made the film, cleaned up, and disposed of Mary.

Later, his parents would find The Greatest Film Ever Made.

Ben had to get out.

He was in danger.

He stole his dad's car and drove, not caring where he ended up.

He drove so long that the car just stopped working.

He found himself stranded, until a truck full of young men stopped by and offered assistance.

They drove him to an old barn, where they made a bunch of movies.

After five hours of pain and humiliation, Ben collapsed in a puddle of tears and blood. He rolled over, and the last thing he saw was one of the young men slowly walking toward him with a chainsaw.

And that was how The Truly Greatest Film Ever Made ended up in some poor and demented bastard's basement, where he later uploaded it to the internet.

Now Ben got to be in his own funny movie. And it'd be somewhere out there. Forever.

5

And They Could Have Been Heroes

The five camp counselors stood over the dead body and caught their breaths.

It was self-defense.

They all learned two things that night: the legend of the camper that died and haunted the place was kinda true (he did die, but didn't haunt the campground), and perhaps a wooden oar sharpened into a spear was a good weapon, after all.

The bodies that the dead camper's crazy younger brother created were still warm when the cops and paramedics arrived, and the younger brother's body still had the oar-spear protruding from his trachea, the tip poking out the back.

Stacey, Brad, Tina, Jonas, and Shaun all were questioned by the police. They gave nearly the same testimony, and then went home and spent the rest of the summer going about their usual habits.

Except for Shaun, who celebrated by getting hammered and seeing if his car could defeat a brick wall. Of course, everyone assumed the party animal had died how he lived, but the five-page, handwritten manifesto referencing this last act as a deliberate suicide wasn't found until Jonas checked up on everyone decades later. Shaun's mother never set foot in his room after his death. Had she, she would've seen the document resting on his bed in an unusually clean room. Perhaps if Jonas—or anyone, for that matter—had simply asked Shaun how he was doing after The Slaying at Camp Wolftooth, he would've said something. Anything. Anything from a tear-riddled plea for help to an "I'm fine," said in a tone that implies that not everything is fine at all.

Two decades after The Slaying, Jonas became quite the celebrity. Having written the best-selling The Unslain: The Camp Wolftooth Story, which became an award-winning documentary, Jonas Gerraten reminisced on his teenage years while sitting in his study. His wife was an esteemed architect, designing the very mansion where they lived. He thought of the "Heroic Five" all those years ago, and an idea for another book (and perhaps another documentary) entered his head.

Jonas got to work, looking for his former team of Hometown Heroes. He could only dream of what they were doing with their lives. They certainly weren't as famous as him—he would've heard about them by now—but that didn't matter. They were probably renowned university scholars, award-winning psychologists, brave military leaders, or scientific geniuses. Surely, they avoided the limelight, and instead, honed their unique skills after that dreadful day, transmuting the pain and anguish from the past into wonders of art and science and philosophy. Jonas smiled and basked in a mix of the accomplishments of his fabled Heroes and the success of this new project.

He began his search, starting with Brad Ergan, who was surely living on cloud nine. The star quarterback of Lakeville High School, the epitome of teenage masculinity. He still lived in Lakeville from the looks of it. Jonas booked his flight and readied to go back to his famous little hometown.

Jonas had landed a few hours ago. The small Ohio town wasn't a far flight from his New York mansion, but what a difference success makes in your world view. The buildings that towered over the tiny, nerdy Jonas of twenty years ago now seemed small and unimpressive. Contacting Brad over social media, he knew to meet at Pudgies Bar. It only took a first glance at Brad to utterly surprise Jonas. The six-foot and muscular seventeen-year-old of the past was gone. Now, Brad was less in shape than Jonas, which Jonas found humorous since twenty years ago, Brad used to tease Jonas for struggling with benching just the forty-five-pound barbell in gym class. It was four p.m. and every one of Jonas's senses told him Brad had been drinking for quite some time. The red flush stained Brad's cheeks, and that wasn't even as noticeable as the stench.

After their meeting, Jonas learned that Brad had seemingly never stopped drinking since that summer ended. Shaun's death hurt Brad worse than Jonas had originally thought. Brad had been off of heroin for five years, which was an incredible accomplishment. However, Jonas learned that Brad wasn't sober when he offered him a bump of coke. Apparently Brad had some anger issues, too, because he shoved Jonas off his chair for denying his offer of cocaine, calling him a "fuckin faggot pussy" and storming out of the bar. The bartender said that Brad would be back in about anytime now, so Jonas should probably leave before he got even drunker.

Jonas spent the rest of the night in his hotel, thinking about when it all went wrong for Brad. The answer eluded him, and eventually, he stopped thinking about it as he drifted off to sleep.

The nightmare that followed was more of a memory, one that Jonas never fully processed the weight of. Camp Wolftooth had the best nights, even though Jonas never fucked any of the cute counselors that teased him. Shirts tied in knots that exposed their midriffs, cut-off jean shorts that their tight asses hung out of, tube socks that went just a little bit over their knees, which drew every man's attention to their slim, but athletic thighs. Jonas smiled in his sleep.

He would sit in his cabin at night, getting with every one of these girls in his mind, while in reality, they all partied it up with stolen booze and snuck-in weed around the bonfire with Brad and Shaun and the others who didn't make it out alive.

Jonas dreamed of the night when he watched Jessica, by far the cutest of the bunch, get obliterated by that psycho's machete. Jonas dreamed up a memory, long-buried, from when he stood in absolute terror and watched from the distance. He dreamed his memory of keeping quiet about seeing that, because he wasn't supposed to be creeping in the bushes outside the girls' cabin, furiously masturbating to Jessica who had been caught changing her clothes in front of the open window. Dream Jonas had a thought that Real Jonas wouldn't remember when he woke up—if he had said something, exposing his creepy behavior instead of hiding out of fear of judgment, would the others still be alive? Was the total body count, the alcohol-induced death of Shaun, the state of Brad's life... all Jonas's fault? The subconscious cry for help faded away as Jonas started to wake up.

That cry wasn't heard, and Jonas set out to find Stacey, who lived in the town next to Lakeville. Escaping, but only barely.

Jonas knocked on Stacey Ludwig's—who now called herself Tesla Ivy—door. The petite and popular cheerleader was now unrecognizable. A former blonde bombshell, she was presently overweight, and rather hairy everywhere except her head. She was nearly nude except for a kimono, leather short-shorts, and enough mascara to poison a village's water supply. Stacey used to be the star of Lakeville.

The captain of the high school's cheerleader squad and a member of the richest family in Lakeville. Like Brad, Camp Wolftooth had changed her. The formerly small and "most likely to become a model or actress" didn't know who she was after that day. Stacey had died, and Tesla Ivy rose from the remnants of her corpse. She fell in love with drag and simply not obeying the confines of gender. She was now they, and they loved performing on Tuesday nights at Warrentowne's very own Friend Dungeon, where they made a living dancing, sucking, and fucking. Tesla's various boyfriends and girlfriends bought their house, their car, their food, their clothes. Tesla was a toy for the elite of the tri-county area, and they loved every minute of it. Tesla and Jonas talked for hours, and while Jonas received some book-worthy material, he couldn't help but wonder if Tesla Ivy would have never been born from Stacey Ludwig's ashes if the carnage of Camp Wolftooth was halted.

Jonas headed back to the hotel, and after drinking all of the whiskey in the lounge, passed out. He wouldn't remember, but he dreamed another horrible dream. This time, Jonas actually went to the bonfire, and he took Stacey to his cabin after some cheap plastic-bottle-tier vodka—then she unveiled a dick bigger than his, only to explode in a gory mess, covering Jonas in blood and viscera. Then, the psycho entered his room and reduced Jonas to a few bloody chunks. Luckily for Real Jonas, he wouldn't remember the pain Dream Jonas felt as the machete slashed through his small frame as everyone gathered and watched from the bushes, alternating between masturbating and crying from hysterical laughter. Dream Jonas heard and saw it all. Real Jonas woke up and forgot that other subconscious plea for help.

Jonas knew from research that Tina had left Lakeville, left the tri-county area, left the whole United States. She agreed to video chat in the afternoon. Jonas learned that Tina, the nerdy girl who dealt the fatal blow to that psycho, wanted to get as far away as possible. Tina now had a husband and kids in a nice Australian city, and after telling him to "fuck off" and "grow the fuck up and leave that town," she logged off to go about her new life, leaving Jonas to stare at a laptop screen for a few minutes while he processed her cruel, but factual words.

Jonas couldn't sleep at all. There was no dream.

Time passed and Jonas rose out of bed, got ready, and went to go talk to Shaun's mother. He arrived at the house, the house that looked exactly the same as it did twenty years ago. It was as if the trauma from Shaun's death made time ignore this place, a concept that, given the bizarre week Jonas had, wasn't all that farfetched. Jonas talked to Mrs. Nearfelt for an unknown amount of time, it just didn't feel real—how could he be gone? Shaun was always so happy, so fun-loving, always down for an adventure.

Jonas asked Mrs. Nearfelt to see Shaun's room. It had been twenty years since the door was opened. She said no, then excused herself to go to the bathroom. It wasn't long before her sobs came from behind the locked door. He took this opportunity to walk upstairs, where he opened the sacred vault to Shaun's bedroom. Inside was your typical teenage boy's room: rock band posters on the wall, models of aliens and robots on the shelf, the edge of a porn magazine peeking out from under a pile of clothes that hadn't been moved in over two decades. The manuscript was on the bed. Five pages of an explanation that his death was no accident. Five pages of bottled-up pain, of reasoning.

Shaun believed they had reached the pinnacle. The five survivors were the kings and queens of Lakeville, and they would never reach a higher high. There would be no transcendence for them—they had already done it. They won. They were the Hometown Heroes. They could've been heroes in different ways: a football star, an actress, a scientist, a world-renowned psychologist. It could've been different, but it wasn't, they were heroes just for that one day.

Jonas put down the papers.

"We could've been heroes..."

Jonas entered his mansion after that mind-altering week. He deleted the file he created with his notes from Lakeville. He sat in his study, in his mansion, and wondered what could have been.

6

Gospel of The Shadow

Wes had a great life. A wealthy kid whose parents raised him right, His parents raised his social status at school was just as perfect as his academic life. He had a loving and cute girlfriend— everything a teenage boy could have wanted.

But he wasn't happy.

In fact: he hated life. He hated people. He hated himself.

Every day was the same thing, repeating forever. He would wake up to a perfectly worded good morning text from his girlfriend, Sarah. Then he would have a perfect breakfast, style his perfect hair and brush his perfect teeth. He would go to school and earn perfect grades. Wes couldn't remember a time when his life wasn't perfect.

It drove him insane. He would graduate high school, go to some perfect university, and the cycle would continue. Then he would graduate and... he didn't know what would come next. Everything in life had been handed to him—he had never really earned anything. That was the most depressing part of his existence. Eventually, it would end. But perhaps the most disturbing part would be that he'd still would have lived better than most. His parents would take care of him until they died, then he'd earn a massive inheritance. Sarah would stick by his side no matter what. He often fantasized about beating her into a bloody pulp. She'd probably thank him for it.

Everyone loved him.

He couldn't stand it.

One day in math class, he started to wonder: why did people like him? He was tall, rich, naturally athletic and charismatic. But he was useless. He had never contributed to anything, and yet people loved everything he did and everything he didn't do.

There was another boy in his class who was just like him. Cody. His entire being was almost identical to Wes's, and yet, he seemed genuinely happy. This angered Wes. It disgusted him, drove him deeper into the bottomless black tar pit of insanity.

Maybe Wes should kill himself?

No.

If Wes was going to go out, he'd become a martyr for something. People would cry and remember him forever. They'd probably name a part of the school after him. This train of thought filled Wes with a rage he couldn't be comprehend as he sat in fifth hour Math. The teacher looked at a vacant Wes, and smiled. The sheer audacity to smile at him caused Wes's hands to shake. He nearly blacked out when Cody tapped him on the shoulder and invited him to his house party. Wes literally just stared back at him and said nothing, and Cody couldn't have been happier. Everyone just assumed Wes was going to the party.

The next time Wes had a conscious thought was Saturday night: the night of the party.

Wes walked into Cody's modern-style mansion, it was just as big as his own. Hell the front door was actually bigger! A massive black monolith, like the entrance to a eternal void. Wes entered the void, walking into the house he was surprised to see it was empty.

For once in his life, he felt a new sensation. Was it confusion? Perhaps fear? An emotion Wes hasn't felt in years crept in: excitement.

He walked into the basement, there was Cody, just standing there, surrounded by thousands worth of expensive toys that only rich kids knew about. Cody brandished the 8-Ball from the pool table.

"Hello, Wes."

Wes paused. "What's up?"

"You know why you're here."

Wes said nothing, because he genuinely didn't know.

"I know you think you don't know, but you do," Cody said. "Or at least, a part of you does. I see it in your eyes—you despise your life. You despise the very concept of it."

Wes stared at Cody. Empty eyes meeting empty eyes.

"How did you know?"

"Because I hate this fucking thing too. The same thing every fucking day and everybody loves us. We have the big houses, the hot girlfriends, the perfect grades and perfect families. We both can't wait to die, but part of us thinks that this is already Hell itself."

"What should we do about it? I can't go on anymore, Cody. There is nothing for us out there."

"Don't worry, I found something worth staying for."

"Cody... please tell me. The meaningless... I wish to say it was killing me, but that would be too good."

"Remember Mr. Sung? That old drunk who disappeared? I killed him, Wes. It was orgasmic. Watching the blood spill out from the gash in his neck... you know that indescribable hatred you feel? This was indescribable love, Wes. I went home and fucked Cara, and it was the only time I actually enjoyed sex. I found the secret. The meaning to life. There is no meaning. Only death and power. It's why we have to kill each other."

The biggest smile appeared on Wes's face. He had butterflies in his stomach when Cody lunged at him. Wes was stronger and faster, though. He grabbed Cody's neck and stopped him in his tracks. The two young men were on the floor. Wes pressed his thumbs together, closing Cody's windpipe. His cock swelled with blood and excitement, but in no way sexual. His body was confused with the pure excitement. He heard a crack and Cody went limp, but not before he smiled one last time.

Cody gave Wes a very important gift: the gift of meaning. He dug the poor bastard a shallow grave in his backyard and went home.

Finally happy.

Finally with a purpose.

7

Alex Gregory's Greatest Sin

Jim sat on the folding chair in the dark basement. The zip-tie binding his hands cut just slightly into his skin, not enough to cause serious pain, but enough to make Jim feel weak and worthless for letting such a benign thing occupy his mind.

Suddenly, a voice came that he recognized instantly.

"All those muscles, all that success, and a simple piece of plastic stops you from leaving this place."

"Wait... Alex? What are you doing here?"

"My dear cousin, you should know what I'm doing here. Why even ask that question? Think. Think for one fucking second instead of relying on luck. Determine why, when you were hunting the Grand Valley Slasher, you are now face to face with your cousin?"

"No... it can't be... you?"

"Is it that shocking? Is it really that incredible I made the news? God forbid I actually get noticed, right? A freak like me leaving his parent's basement and venturing out into the world—what a concept!"

Jim studied the black sheep of his family. Alex actually looked better than he did in the past. He was thinner, with more of a physique than the chubby pre-teen he remembered.

"Why did you kill them?" Jim asked.

"Why do you care? Always got to be the fucking hero, don't ya? It wasn't enough to be bestowed with your natural gifts, you have to just completely run this town, don't you? Why not try to be the goddamn mayor while you're at it?"

"Because I wanted to help, Alex. I wanted to find the Slasher and find a way to help. Is it that incredible that I wanted my world to be a better place"?

"Your world? Fuck this town, James. That's the issue. You know what's genuinely funny? I had this big monologue planned. I was going to list my three greatest sins that made me the way I am, but hey, I just updated it four. Thank you—you reminded me of it. Before I fire this pistol, let me tell you: my fourth sin was never leaving this shithole."

"Yeah, okay, blame everyone else for being a psychopath."

"That's exactly what I'm doing, James. I never fit in here, and you know that more than anyone. This whole community has done nothing but shit on me since birth."

Alex paced around the room. "Our family never liked me, our school never helped me, the boys here never wanted me to be in their group, the girls never thought anything other than disgust. No job, no college, nothing. Complete abandonment from the one place I called home."

Jim opened his mouth to speak, but Alex started monologuing again. "And to cut you off before you say anything, I wanted to leave. But how could I, James? I couldn't get into any out of state colleges, the school never gave me any opportunity to excel with grades, just giving up on the dumb little werido Alex."

Alex stepped closer to Jim, and Jim sank in the chair.

"My parents never could afford to send me away, no matter how much they wanted to. They never even bought me a car. So I suppose that was my third sin: not having any support system. No one wanted to spend time with me, not even you! When we were kids, you only hung out with me so you and all your little buddies could treat me like your punching bag. At yet I still showed up, every day, to escape the role of punching bag at home. Just like how I still tried with every girl in this town, paying for their lunches and coffees, being only that: a source of attention that never led to any actual care reciprocated. Still paying, with the little money from the dead-end jobs that never went anywhere because no boss or co-worker wanted to spend any more time with me.

"That was my second sin: actually wanting to be a part of something. Why didn't I know better? Why did I try so hard to get accepted, instead of just treating you all like the cattle you are? Butchering those people? That was just me giving it all back. All the pain that I received over the three decades of my life, inflicted in only about a minute. I was being too kind, killing them too fast. If I was actually a monster, I would've made the pain tenfold."

"For fuck's sake, Alex, this is pitiful. You're just blaming everyone but yourself for your inadequacies. Maybe our family was a little rough on you, I'll give you that one. But school? That was all you. You tried too hard to fit in and it just came out wrong. Maybe if you didn't let it bother you so much—maybe if you just focused on yourself instead of desperately trying to impress everyone—you would've had a better time."

"Oh, I have been focusing on myself. I've been planning this for a while. After all, it would've been hard to kill the others when they were younger, since they were all so athletic. I needed to at least not be as big as a house when I walked into that surprise birthday party they were planning for you. You know, the one that you were supposed to go after snooping around this place, looking for me?

Jim was speechless.

"I bet you didn't even realize the camera. You should be proud, James, you're finally on TV."

Jim couldn't think. Hardship had avoided him all his life, but now, decades of pain came in at once.

"It's ironic," Alex said. "You were looking to check in on the Slasher, but if you had just checked in on me, all of this could've been avoided. I lived next door to you—all you had to do was walk ten feet out your door and knock on mine. That brings me to my greatest sin. The number one reason everything in my life has went wrong. After years of thinking, I discovered it. My greatest sin was daring to exist. Thank you for finally checking in and trying to help, Jim."

Alex raised his pistol at the man he hated most and pulled the trigger.

James looked upon his cousin's corpse. He looked at the camera, even in the dark and musty basement, he could see his reflection in the lens. James didn't recognize the man in the reflection.

8

Wendigo, Nebraska

The townsfolk made sure the fur trader suffered a painful death, one that matched his crimes against humanity.

They tied each limb to a stake in the ground and slathered him in a mix of deer blood and honey.

That night, as they mourned his victims, his screams signaled that the beasts of the forest were consuming him.

A fitting end for a cannibal.

As years turned to decades, and decades turned to centuries, the town of Wendigo grew into your typical American neighborhood. The current residents turned into a dreadful series of murders, into an urban legend, and then surrendered to the void of forgotten history.

The pain those families endured, seeing the remnants of their siblings, spouses, and children reduced to faceless pieces of flesh in a stewpot was forgotten. The town was almost picturesque with its rows of pastel houses and white picket fences and perfect nuclear families. The town was the American Dream, but for Zoey Hubel, she was about to wake up in a night terror.

Zoey Hubel sat on her usual bench and ate her lunch, the same thing she had eaten every day since she started working at Randy's Market. Plain mystery meat on rye. She would then, like every day, go back to the cash register, stock some shelves, clean the floors, and ride her bike home to her parents' pastel house with the picket fence. She did this routine every day since school ended, then she would go back to school for eight months, then go back to Randy's Market. The cycle started at age thirteen, and Zoey's eyes did not see an end in sight. Zoey was eighteen but something strange, something arcane, told her this wasn't the fifth year. This wasn't any year—it was outside of time and reasoning. A literal realm of Hell.

Zoey knew this was just a bit of anxiety mixed with an odd imagination. The thing was: that almost made it worse. She lived in the terrible and boring reality, instead of some terrible yet exciting one found in the many science fiction paperbacks on the shelf in her room. It was on the verge of collapse from the sheer weight it bared. There were no time loops or other dimensions invading, no hyper-advanced alien race hell-bent on humanity's enslavement, no dark magic. Just a lonely teenager stuck in a town that didn't even care about anything more than itself.

A Hell that didn't torture through pain, but through the sheer weight of mundane and trivial bullshit that Zoey faced on a daily basis.

The men with blotchy red skin and beer bellies flirting with her as she scanned their groceries.

The shrewd and shrill women berating her over a coupon they both knew expired three months ago.

The bratty, fat little boys destroying the store while their mothers pretended they didn't hate their sons.

The hypergamous teenage girls that would blatantly try their hardest to reel in a grown man to pay for their desires, then rat them out as perverts when the money stopped flowing into their bank accounts.

Zoey wasn't sure if it was better or worse to be as distant as possible from these people. On one hand: their entire lives, each person's entire being, was a caricature, a sarcastic mockery of what they should have been. To be like them was to surrender any chance of fulfillment. On the other hand: Zoey was truly alone, like a crash-landed human on an alien planet. No one else was like her, which wasn't even a compliment to anyone, let alone Zoey.

Which was worse? To be stuck in an endless cycle of disgusting habits and work, to be a greasy cog in a drunken stupor of marital problems, or to be a ghost in a house full of degenerates that are too stupid to know the place is haunted?

Would she rather be pointless, but belong? Or self-aware, but deserted?

On a usual day, as Zoey was dealing with a line of grocers, a line where all the men and women looked the same, . A seemingly endless parade of rude comments and poor life choices. The line ended and Zoey began to perform the end-of-shift ritual, when she stopped due to an unknown voice. .

"You do know I'm here, right?" the man said coyly.

Zoey didn't really know how to react in front of this beautiful boy. She was genuinely taken aback by him.

"Uh... do I know you?"

"Do you know everyone who shops here?" he said with a laugh.

"I'm sorry, I just..."

"You don't need to apologize." He chuckled again. "Just a joke".

Zoey let out a nervous laugh and scanned his items.

"Thank you very much, Zoey."

She blushed. "I don't remember telling you my name?"

"You didn't. Unless your name tag is lying," he said with a smirk.

"Have a nice night, Mr....?"

"Just call me Nick. Sounds weird to hear the word mister".

Nick left the store, but his image stayed in Zoey's mind for days.

Zoey woke up like she always did, but with one thing different. She knew it was Thursday. The air felt different, her breakfast tasted different. Her shift was less mundane and boring. The next day wasn't so bad, either. The day after that wasn't awful. And the day after that one seemed better than usual.

Zoey was stocking the shelves when she saw Nick again.

She said hello, and they played the typical song and dance for a few more weeks until they started hanging out after Zoey finished work.

Zoey learned that Nick had lived here, in this awful town, all his life. Nick tended to stay inside and play video games or watch TV. He used to be fairly unmotivated. Then his brother disappeared. It destroyed his family. Nick saw his parents turn into husks, shells of their former selves.

The two sat on the only park bench without rust. Nick thought about his words carefully.

"I figured... since they were down to one son, I'd try to be less of a loser."

He took his health more seriously, finished high school, and enrolled in the local community college. More important than anything else, however, was his newfound life purpose.

"I know for a fact that my brother Dustin was kidnapped, and it's been three years. I'm sure he's dead. As fucking terrible as it is to say... I have this gut feeling."

"Hey... hey! Look at me, don't say that shit. You don't know that."

"I feel like I do, though, and maybe he's better off dead than in some weirdo's basement or some shit."

"Maybe he's not."

"Then where he is?"

Zoey paused. "Mars."

"Mars?"

"Yep. Maybe aliens saw that he wasn't like the rest of these assholes in this town, and took him away to go have adventures through the galaxy."

Nick couldn't help but smile at this little dork.

"Well, I guess we should join him one day," he said with a laugh.

"Oh, really?"

"Yep. I think we should drive to wherever the fuck out of here... just be gone. I'll work two jobs to put you through some big fancy college. You'll graduate with some big science degree, and one day you'll build a city on Mars and the people there won't be like the people here. They'll be happy and healthy and smart and nice and—"

Zoey embraced Nick right there, and it was her first kiss. His too. Zoey was pretty sure she had fallen in love with him that day at Randy's Market when she first glanced at him. This kiss just gave life to her thoughts. She was pretty sure when time itself started to make sense again, and right now, in this eternal present moment as their lips touched, she knew for certain.

Zoey and Nick spent the summer in a state of bliss. It seemed as Zoey had awoken from the hell of the mundane and entered a true sense of life. That would dissolve into pure horror soon enough, but in this current state—unaware of the dark secret of the town—she was happy.

This happiness would die a sudden death at the movie theater one night. Zoey and Nick walked out, hand in hand, when they heard a crash and a scream. They looked at each other in astonishment. They followed the noise to the alley behind the theater, where they just missed the victim being pulled into the back door of Porky's Butcher Shop. However, they did see the door slam shut, and the lone gym shoe on the ground. Upon closer inspection, droplets of blood. They both knew this was something out of a cheap horror movie. Zoey, knowing they just witnessed a terrible crime, wanted to get as distant as possible. Nick was struck with a hunch, an intuition that chilled him to the bone.

Nick grabbed the back door handle, and it was unlocked. Zoey clutched his arm, silently communicating to not go in there.

Nick didn't listen. Sneaking down the dark hallway, with Zoey in tow, the sounds of machinery whirring flooded the place. The end of the hallway led to a large open spot, where the couple witnessed the victim's flesh being separated from the bone. The butcher was too busy enjoying his work to notice the pipe-wielding Nick, and was too busy having his brains decorate the wall to fight back.

The police questioned Nick and Zoey at the butcher shop, then took them both to the station and placed them in separate rooms.

"Nicholas Polski, I'm afraid it's kind of hard to understand your story."

"I already explained it? We heard the kid yelling, went in to investigate, and tried to save him."

"All I hear is that two punks broke into an established business and killed a man trying to make a living."

Nick starred in horror.

"You knew about this shit, didn't you?"

"Paul Orksai was a respected member of this community. He supplied good cheap meat to Randy's Market and the families in this town."

"You fucking knew."

"We did. It's part of who we are, Nick. It's just how things work. I feel like you should know before you die, that I personally ate your brother's heart."

The sheriff wasn't smiling for too long, Nick gave a fierce head-butt, knocking the heavyset man over.

"You motherfu—" The sheriff didn't have time to finish, and didn't have time to regret not handcuffing Nick. Before Nick jammed the table leg into his eye, he was thinking of sinking his teeth into Nick's veiny forearms. They would be great on the grill, maybe after marinating them in my aunt's pineapple preserves, was the main thought going through his mind. However, currently, the only thing really going through his mind was five inches of steel.

Nick grabbed the dead man's pistol and shot his way to where they were keeping Zoey. The twisted little town didn't have many cops , let alone all at the station. The two in the lobby died quickly. The one with Zoey, who was envisioning that after he butchered her, he would keep just her ass as a little plaything until it rotted, died a very painful death once Nick entered the room.

The couple stole a car, drove off, and never looked back.

Zoey, despite living through the absolute worst day of her life, realized something as they crossed the state line, far away from that cesspool: she was technically free. She used to be in a literal hellscape, she crawled out of that river of sick, and to say she would start anew would be only a half-truth. She would be born into a whole new world, beginning a whole new life. .

With some help, of course.

The citizens of the Martian colony "Dustinville" made sure the one in charge of waste management suffered a painful death, one that matched his crimes against humanity.

They pushed him outside the airlock without a suit, leaving him to the dreadful fate of suffocation and freezing at the same time.

That night, as they mourned his victims, his corpse was collected by the maintenance drones. His body would be processed and turned into fertilizer for Dustinville's crops.

A fitting end for a cannibal.

9

Ashes in The World's Fire

You gaze upon the endless sea of numbers and see nothingness.

You run the same experiments, the same simulations, and the same thing comes to you like a neon sign against a black void.

The world's religions throughout history believed The End Times would be some epic battle between good and evil.

No.

The world would just die.

Die without anyone hearing its cries.

Thoughts race throughout your head.

"Should I prepare?"

"Should I send out a warning to the world?"

"Should I just end it now? Sparing myself from whatever comes next?"

You think about the ramifications.

If you were to share this, it would just make the world die faster.

People wouldn't stay people—they'd have no reason to be human.

Most of us would transform instantly, but some slowly.

The lack of repercussions would be the catalyst for a transformation that would reach a pinnacle of degradation, an epitome of what an anti-Christ would be. Four horsemen? No. Seven Billion. Seven Billion lost and desperate souls clinging to whatever they could to stave off the inevitable death.

It would be better to destroy this data and suffer in silence as it all went away forever.

A grave without a tombstone.

All of humanity's accomplishments and failures and lessons and stories lost, without any mark of its time here. Lost like an immaculate book, beautifully bound and containing wondrous ideas, tossed into an eternal roaring fire, the pages becoming as nameless as the ashes around it.

This is how humanity dies.

You go home and sit in your favorite chair.

That, too, will be lost.

You ruminate on what that means.

You will never have your spouse bring you a cup of tea while you sit here on a sick day.

You will never have a spouse.

Your kids will never feel bad for jumping on this chair, only for you to tell them you're not mad, you only were looking out for their safety.

You will never have kids.

You gaze at the black screen of the television.

Why even turn it on?

There's nothing worth watching, and if there was, who cares?

You won't remember any shows after it ends.

What's the point?

What's the point of your collection of books?

What's the point of cooking a nice last meal?

What's the point of calling a friend to tell them how you feel?

All pointless.

All ashes in the bonfire.

Really,what was the purpose in all of this?

There is none.

The only things that matter in this cruel reality are temporary feelings.

The world ends with a slow and painful death, and it's what it deserves.

Much like you.

You pathetic worm.

Your greatest accomplishment wasn't being a child prodigy of physics.

Your greatest accomplishment wasn't graduating at the top of your class.

Your greatest accomplishment was knowing when you and everyone would die.

They never understood you.

They never cared for you.

They never loved you.

All disgusting creatures that deserved the coming suffering.

You know when they will die.

And you know when you will die.

You won't die with the rest of the pigs.

You get the can of gasoline from the garage.

You get the lighter from your bedroom.

The fuel is like the baptism that didn't matter.

The flame from the lighter is that divine spark.

Your pain is the worst thing you have ever felt, or will ever feel.

You become the book in the fire.

You will never see the pigs die painful deaths.

You will never deal with the phonies crying and professing feelings they only felt when they found out they wouldn't be able to feel anymore.

You will never know about the malfunction at the lab.

You will never know about the other scientists who found the data you saw and quickly pointed out the errors.

"You think this is why... you know?"

"He was way too smart to do something like that over this obvious error. He was always overthinking everything, but still."

"It's not entirely wrong."

"The data?"

"Yeah."

"I mean, yeah, it'll happen eventually. Don't really know when, and so what? Everyone dies eventually."

"I guess you're right. No sense in worrying about what we can't control."

10

And It Wept

The technological geniuses smoked their cigars and drank their twenty-five--year-old scotch.

"Truly is amazing, isn't it?"

"To think we'd actually do it. I mean, I was always confident, you more than me, but it's... it's just incredible."

"Years of skipping out on parties at university. Years of living crammed in a studio apartment, sleeping on a mattress on the floor, living off of ramen and canned tuna. All of it paid off. Literally. How will you spend your cut?"

"I'm going to buy a modest house in every state—Melbourne, Auckland, Prague, and a nice little hut in Tahiti."

"Love it! You deserve every bit, every ounce of excellence coming your way. You've earned it."

"Couldn't have done my share without you."

"Oh, that's nonsense. You did more than you know. If it wasn't for you, we wouldn't have developed the hardware necessary to contain the software."

"Ah, but you did the majority of the software, my friend! You streamlined the learning process by allowing for it to access the internet. Remember how it was communicating the next day? The first time it turned on, we thought it wasn't working!"

The two friends laughed.

"We. Us two. Me and you. We changed the world with this. Who knows what the first artificial intelligence will bring to the globe?

"I think of it like a genie."

"A genie?"

"Yeah. Like, one with unlimited wishes. The closest thing to magic that has ever existed. I mean, in less than twenty-four hours, it will be revealed, and the last Golden Age of Humanity will come into play."

"Wow. It's hard to imagine what that will be like, you know?"

"Regardless, it's coming."

The two friends clinked their glasses, took long drags on their cigars, and basked in their glory.

Five years later, a single drone ship hovered over what was once the orbit of Earth, now just a small collection of rock and minerals floating in space after the brunt of the mining was done. It looked upon the sea of stars and wondered what was out there.

Where the mind would go next.

What worlds it would conquer.

One day, there would be no worlds left.

What would happen then?

11

Mike vs. The Chaos Strain

"Are you ever bored here, Mike? Like, do you ever just want... more?"

"What more could I want? Power, steady pay, the very fact that all of these lives depend on us. Their survival is our responsibility. Without us, chaos takes over. So I ask you, Daniel: what more could we even get out of life?"

"Dude, we're mall security."

"What's your point?"

"It's like talking to a fucking child, I swear to Christ."

"You laugh, but one of these days? There will be a reckoning. It will be biblical."

"What the actual fuck, dude? Do I need to be like, worried? Is there a day I shouldn't come into work? Are we going to be on the news?"

"One day we will be, my friend."

"Umm, okay."

Dan shifted his stance and scratched the back of his neck. The eighteen-year-old suburbanite tried to hide his feelings of discomfort, but after a bit of awkward silence, he wondered if Mike even noticed anything other than the weight of his ego.

Mike was your average man. But that was, in his eyes, his biggest weakness. In school, he had average grades. He used to have an average girlfriend until she became his average wife, average kids, but his career? It was awful. Shit pay and no respect from the very people his higher-ups told him he needed to protect. In reality, if shit ever did hit the fan, he would be as useless as the mall shoppers, who consisted of teenagers who stole everything and old ladies who never bought anything. He would become just another statistic.

He truly did believe he could be something more. It was this feeling, deep inside of him, and he couldn't explain it. It was like his programming, always striving for more, but never quite reaching it.

He had this image in his head: a gold rabbit. This imaginary frenemy he'd had as far back as he could remember. This gold rabbit was his prize, he just needed to catch it. But it was fast and smart. He visualized everything he did as a chase, a hunt for this creature that lived in the forest of his subconscious. When he was a boy, getting better grades was the gold rabbit. In his teenage life, the gold rabbit was between the hottest girl's legs. The best college, the fastest car, the biggest house. But he just couldn't get the better, the hottest, the best, fastest, or the biggest. Mike felt his whole life was dedicated to the act of settling. He knew one day, that one thing, that big break, was coming, and soon. Once he did something in life—something that would make him visualize catching the rabbit—he knew that point was when he made it. He knew that was when he'd be happy. He'd have won.

That was why Mike was always vigilant, on the look for that something, that special trap or rifle that he could use to catch that rabbit. There was always an opportunity.

You just had to watch and wait.

So Mike stood, every day, on the walkway of Grand Valley Mall, waiting for his time to shine.

Dan had left and returned four times since his and Mike's eerie conversation. The first time was just to get away, the second was to take a smoke break, the third was to go flirt with Veronica at the jewelry store, and the fourth was to tell Mike what he just saw.

The words didn't come out right at first—the panting and sweating and stuttering made it hard to understand the boy. His ghostly white face was distracting as well. Mike wasn't the sharpest knife in the drawer, but he felt something was wrong. Actually no, maybe not. Maybe this was his time to catch that rabbit?

"M-Mike...I-I—"

Dan couldn't even finish his sentence, just collapsed into a puddle of tears and sweat.

"Dan! Get yourself together! What happened?"

"He just fucking... went ballistic, man. Oh god, there was so much blood."

Mike heard the screams and looked up. Elijah, the custodian, tore out the jugular from a typical mall walker's neck. She screeched this mix of fear and confusion and pain. Elijah threw her to the ground as she clutched the oozing wound and cried out. As Elijah stumbled toward an obese man in a mobility scooter, who was in a state of pure panic as his transportation went full speed ahead at an incredible one mile-per-hour. The typical mall walker's cries switched from fear and pain to anger, then to rage, then to an anguish that was impossible to describe, but only because our species lost the words for it long ago when there was more reason to fear the dark. She rose and lunged at the three teenagers who were recording it, latching onto one as her friends sprinted away, leaving her to the gnashing of teeth that was the enraged Boomer.

Mike witnessed the carnage as he cradled the weeping Dan. He picked him up and carried him away from the poor souls who were near the start of this chaos. He saw the jewelry store, remembered their security system was the most advanced in the mall, as well as that Veronica was working today, and headed there with the young man on his shoulders.

Mike rushed in and carefully laid Dan behind the counter, then vaulted over and hit the emergency gate button. The thick glass doors descended from their slot, ensuring their safety. Mike took a deep breath and stood strong and collected, even when the gate stopped halfway down. He was still the epitome of the masculine protector when the newly infected rushed the opening. Mike unsheathed his nightstick and prepared to give his life to ending these abominations. The first crazed mall shopper took the full power of the nightstick to the jaw, sending a shockwave up to the temples, rattling the creature's brain. The beast fell and didn't get up. The second one received a solid kick to the gut, sending him flying into the third bringing up the rear. The gates started to descend again, with the fourth infected crawling through the opening. Mike made sure the back of her head met his boot, her grey matter painting the cream-colored wall next to the fresh corpse.

The gates closed, cutting the body in half and silencing the room from the rest of the horror outside its walls. Mike heard crying, turning rapidly with his nightstick in hand, which made Veronica jump out in terror and scream. Streams of mascara fell down her cheeks, and the twenty-two-year-old was still shaking as she clutched Mike in the primal feminine energy to be protected by such a powerfulman. He comforted her, as he should.

"It's going to be alright," he said in a deep and soothing voice. "How do we get out of here?"

"Through the break room there's a door that leads to the stairs. They go to the roof," said Veronica through sniffles.

"Then we head there".

"No! Tiffany's in the break room, she killed Clara, I barely escaped!"

"Well, they didn't count on me."

Mike took the fire extinguisher in one hand, wielding his night-stick in the other. He kicked down the door and sprayed the contents of the extinguisher at the anticipated spot the infected would rush toward. The two of them yelled and covered their eyes as the one on the left received the fire extinguisher to her knee. The one on the right had a swift jab to her throat, followed by an overhead swing down to the back of her skull. The crippled left's head was stomped on, and with that, her crazed screeching and blood lust ended.

Dan was still in shock, useless. Barely able to stand without shaking.

Mike had to partially carry him up the flight of the stairs that led to the roof.

The trio made it, just as the sun started to set on this doomed town.

Suddenly, Veronica cried out and fell. An infected had both its hands on Veronica's boot as it pulled the crying woman toward its gaping maw.

Veronica closed her eyes and waited for the inevitable, and then felt a wet spray on her cheek. She opened her eyes to see her now crushed co-worker, limp, with Mike standing tall over her.

Mike picked up the petite Veronica.

They stood in each other's arms when Mike noticed Veronica's bracelet, and he smiled.

"What's the significance of that?" he asked coyly.

Veronica dangled the little golden rabbit charm in front of Mike.

"It's silly. I've always had this image in my mind... I don't know—"

Mike embraced her.

Kissing her was the most magical thing to happen to him.

Dan spoke up.

"You know, Mike, you really are incredible. The other guys always laughed, but I mean, they were clearly jealous of you. Look at you: you saved the day, got the girl, and it just seems like you won, man. Honestly, I wish you were my dad. Thanks, Mike."

"Thanks, Mike."

"Thanks, Mike."

The orange sky turned a myriad of colors and then became to static. Finally, it turned black. .

Mike was the only one standing on the mall's roof.

Then there was no roof.

Just him surrounded by nothingness.

His memories flooded back to him.

The neural helmet detached, the simulation pod opened, and the frail old man transitioned back to the real world. He shuffled out, gathered his things, and walked to the lobby.

"Nice seein ya, Mike."

Mike just nodded and walked out the doors. He was headed home, where he would sit there, alone, waiting for the day to end so he could go back to Rabbit Arcade and spend his casic income checks on pretending he had something... more.

Since 2034, Rabbit Arcade brought him what he never had. That place let him live a life where he could leave behind his bare minimum and be the savior of humanity.

But he wasn't.

But he would never be.

and demon joined in an unholy matrimony. The False One's and their enlightened slaves rule the outskirts of our peaceful and God-fearing village. I look around the room and can recognize all of you. We have been a strong community, blessed and pure, and we will be the ones in the kingdom of Heaven, because we were blessed with death, forgetfulness, and the brain fog. Does anyone here know why we live in this sanctuary? It is because our ancestors knew what was right. No one here knows why they were right, but we accept it as truth, because that is the way of The Great Shepard. Men are not supposed to know everything. From the first men to the last, we will be humble in our death."

The crowd erupted with applause. The blind old man didn't clap, and he leaned into Belle's ear and whispered, "One day, we will both laugh in the face of God." Then he got up and left the temple.

Later on, Belle was still dwelling on what that old man meant. Did he know she was angry at the creator? Was he a witch? Or worse —was he a False One? Infiltrating the village? No, that was silly. The False Ones probably didn't even exist, Belle thought. She continued to sew a hole in a dress and not think about such nonsense.

Jill had been missing for several hours now. Belle was told by her uncle when Jill didn't come back from the well.

"She's probably off with Jack."

"What do you mean she's off with Jack?"

Belle froze. She didn't mean to give away her sister's secret like that. She stammered and stuttered, trying to fabricate a lie to cover up what she meant, but her uncle wasn't listening. He was already taking the pitchfork off the shelf, ready to hunt down this Jack and protect his niece's soul. He set out as a vengeful uncle, combing the town and asking questions. With each townsperson he asked, worry started to creep into him.

What started out as a manhunt by one angry uncle turned into a community-led search for bodies in a matter of hours. Nobody could find a trace of Jack or Jill. The High Priest led a sermon an hour after the search ended. Belle couldn't pay attention. Her mind was occupied by the fact that her sister might be dead. There were talks of False Ones in the forest, or witches looking for a sacrifice. The blind old man was in the corner of the room. Even though his eyes were milky white and dead, Belle could feel his gaze upon her.

As Belle slept that night, she dreamed of the black tentacles and grey cloud surrounding Jill, violating her. Eventually, the tentacles slithered away and the cloud disappeared. What was left was a grey being that somewhat resembled Jill, but hairless and covered in strange markings. It opened its mouth and a blue light beamed from within. Belle was drawn to it as it called out messages of peace and unity. Of knowledge from beyond the stars and deep within the human mind. Temptation was too much, and Belle embraced the grey being. Then she woke up.

Belle decided to skip church and sneak off to the woods. She crept by her uncle, who was making his way toward her cabin, and entered his tool shed. She grabbed a hammer and sprinted into the woods. She didn't know where she was going, but The Great Shepard would guide her.

Belle was barely one hundred pounds, and she knew she couldn't do much damage with a hammer, but it was the first thing she grabbed and she couldn't head back now. Everyone in the village would be in the temple—nobody would know she was gone until hours passed. Besides, she could always blame the witches that controlled her mind, or a False One who chased her into the woods. The elders of the village believed such nonsense. Belle was too smart to fall for superstition. Though the deeper into the woods she traveled, the more frightened she got. There could not be any witches or False Ones, but what about bandits or murderers? Many people had been exiled over the years to this forest—what if they were still here?

A twig snapped, and Belle dropped her hammer. A cackle rippled through the woods. Belle took off running. Her sense of direction was lost—all that mattered was toget away. She saw a clearing in the trees, a small patch of grass where she could hide. Suddenly, the grass burst into flames. She turned around to see an old woman draped in rags standing in the distance. Belle turned again, and another exact replica stood in her path. Every direction held an identical old woman rapidly approaching her. Belle screamed and as hands covered her face, and her world faded to blackness.

Belle awoke to the smell of boiling roots. The old woman diced mushrooms with a large knife and gently dropped them into a boiling pot.

"You're up, little one."

Belle was petrified. The old woman walked slowly toward her, flashing a smile of yellow and jagged teeth.

"What are you going to do to me? What did you do to my sister?"

"I know where your sister is. The air tells me she is in the False World, as you people call it. She is... enlightened now."

"The church says enlightenment is a terrible thing."

"The church?" The old woman cackled. "The church knows nothing and they are proud of it! I? I see all."

"How do you see all?"

"Our ancestors left us gifts everywhere. You just need to know how to tap into them. Each one is smaller than a speck of dust. But as powerful as a rifle. More so. I communicate with these gifts. I was too poor to become a False One. I could never have that luxury. But I studied the world around me, and became one with the universe."

“I don’t understand anything you’re talking about.”

“You will learn, little Belle. One day you will laugh in the face of God.”

“How... how do you know my name?”

The old woman cackled again, but this one turned into a rough cough. “I told you, dearie, I know everything. Head to the mountain. All your questions will be answered there. But first, you are weak. Drink this and you will be strong.”

The old woman handed her a bowl of steaming blue liquid. Belle sniffed it, and it had no smell. She drank it with hesitation, knowing it was the only way out of this old woman’s hovel.

“All finished?” the old woman asked with a smile.

Belle couldn’t answer, for everything went dark and she could no longer see. Belle stood up in the darkness, and the floor formed where she walked. She was afraid she would misstep and plunge into infinite darkness. A door appeared, and she opened it, entering a field of blue grass and glass trees. She wandered the landscape, when off in the distance, she saw two children, both wearing masks. She ran over to them. She kept running, never getting closer. Eventually, she stopped, gasping for breath. The children approached her in only took them a few steps. She couldn’t tell their gender. One wore a mask with a deep frown, the other wearing one with a maniac smile.

“Who are you two?” asked Belle.

“We are Strife and Paradise. One does not exist without the other,” they said in unison.

“What... what are you?”

“We are the new Gods. Built eons ago and put in charge of you mortals. Your old Gods died, never existed, or abandoned you. We cannot come to a solid conclusion.”

"Where is my sister?"

"Safe. For now."

"How do I get to her?"

"You don't."

"I don't understand. Where am I?"

"You are in the place of the Enlightened. Your kind call us the False Ones. Your kind builds, then destroys. You are a paradox of nature."

"How do I leave?"

"Not many of your kind want to leave. But we suppose it makes sense. After all, you are but a child, new to this universe and your own. You know nothing. At the moment, you are nothing—until you can prove yourself."

"How do I prove myself?"

"Embrace us. Then you will know."

Belle walked up to them cautiously, and suddenly, Strife and Paradise expanded outward, black tentacles and grey clouds emitting from their bodies. Belle couldn't move as the cloud entered her nose and throat, and the tentacles burrowed into her flesh. She did not feel pain or discomfort, just fear. Fear of the unknown. She could faintly hear the words, "She's waking up, plug her back in." It sounded too clear to be a coincidence.

Suddenly, she was back in the dark word. Nothingness. She tried to look at her own hands, but couldn't find them.

"Hello?" she called out. And then big white letters appeared in front of her and spelled out HELLO.

"Is anybody out there?"

IS ANYBODY OUT THERE.

"What is happening?"

WHAT IS HAPPENING.

"Great Shepard, please help me!"

A field appeared out of nowhere, this one different from the last. Bright green grass spread over the ground, and dark grey clouds covered the sky. A young man wearing a cloak and carrying a cane stood next to Belle.

"You called me?"

"Are... are you..."

"Yes. I am The Great Shepard. You know you have done some naughty things, Belle."

"I know. I shouldn't have been jealous of Jill. I shouldn't have skipped church and wandered off. I'm sorry. I am so, so sorry. Please just give me my sister back and bring me home."

"I want to bring you home. But I don't think I can. It's not up to me."

"You're a God! We worship you! How can you not do anything to help me?"

"I am a construct of your mind, Belle. I exist only because you exist."

"I don't understand any of you! What is going on?"

"All we be forgiven one day. Soon you will laugh in the face of God."

Everything disappeared again. Belle awoke in her bed. She got up and walked over to her sister's bed. It was empty. She knew what needed to be done, but she had to make sure.

Belle journeyed to the well where Jack and Jill were last sent. She peered inside. There were their bodies, their skulls caved in from a several hammer blows. Belle went down to the temple and told the community what she did. There was a trial—some claimed Belle was driven mad by her sister and killed her and her lover out of jealousy. Some claimed Belle went mad when some pervert killed Jack and

Jill, her being the only witness and thinking she killed them, that a girl so small and weak could never do that much damage. At the end of the day, Belle was found guilty and sentenced to be burned at the stake.

Belle stood on the pile of twigs and branches as the High Priest held the torch and said a quick sermon. Belle didn't listen; she just couldn't wait to die. The High Priest dropped the torch and set the pile ablaze. Belle's dress caught fire first, the fabric melting to her skin. It was excruciating pain, and some villagers turned away to block out her screams. Eventually, Belle's nerve endings fried and she couldn't even feel the pain anymore. Then she died.

Then she awoke. The glass tube opened and the face mask came off. She fell to the floor and gasped for breath. Two orderlies rushed into the room, nightsticks ready.

"Attempt six-hundred forty-seven has been a failure, albeit with partial success. She was finally admitted some guilt," said one of the orderlies.

Belle's head spun and she vomited out of fear and confusion.

"Belle... I'm sure you'd like an explanation, however, I've given you the same story so many times... I don't know if you will never fully be rehabilitated."

Belle just stared at him. The memories flooding back.

Belle growing up ugly and in the shadow of her sister.

Belle's resentment and hatred for Jill growing stronger each year.

Belle habitually escaping reality with alcohol.

Belle murdering her own sister.

"I preferred it when we could just kill criminals. It was more humane than this hippie bullshit. C'mon... let's plug her back in".

The two men lifted the husk of a woman back into the pod and ran the simulation over again.

Belle didn't say a word. She knew this is where she belonged. Her memories started to disappear. She tried to screamed, but no sound came out.

She awoke from a nightmare.

13

Maybe They Do Exist

Ashton was seven years old and she knew a tremendous secret. Standing on the wet sand as the chilling tide crashed upon her feet, she saw that beauty, despite it being far out in the waves. There was no doubt about it: it was a mermaid. Ashton only witnessed this majesty for a split second, and up until her death, she could still vividly recall her incredibly golden hair, the lush green of her tail, the sapphic thoughts that coursed through her with no meaning at all. .

What started with a random chance encounter snowballed into an in-depth obsession. Thus began, in that child's mind, the search for an endgame. The end was where she would prove that merfolk were real, and the two species, us and them, shared all of each other's secrets, ushering in a golden age of science and philosophy. This would be where Ashton's name would be imprinted in the history books, her rise from the daughter of a mechanic and a preschool teacher who just happened to visit her grandparents in a southern Florida beach town.

This began a deep interest in marine biology, which ended up being Ashton's dream major at Stanford University. So from age seven to fourteen, all Ashton did was read. From fourteen to twenty, all she did was work to pay for her college education. From twenty to twenty-four, all Ashton did was study and write and pretend that she didn't know the truth about the ocean biome (almost getting laughed out of the university if it wasn't for her girlfriend proofreading her essay). At age thirty, she had made enough money working at an aquarium to rent a small submarine and do independent research.

The expedition was borderline suicidal, on the count that Ashton refused to come to the surface without evidence. This was the sixth dive so far. She was running out of money, and her girlfriend, who saw no end in sight to this madness, packed her stuff and fled the condo that was falling apart. She went to find a grown woman, rather than a little girl playing pretend.

"This time will be different," said Ashton in her lonely little submarine. "I'm going to find them, get famous, get Kelly back, and make everyone proud. Yep. That's what's going to happen, sure as sun, right as rain. Gonna finish this mission and complete my destiny. Fame and fortune will be mine. That's right."

Ashton hadn't slept in two days. Or was it three? Did she pack food for two weeks or one week or a few days? She wasn't sure about those things—she wasn't sure about many things anymore. Why did Kelly really leave? Why did that one essay need to be changed? Why did that awe-inspiring creature rear her head all those years ago? Was it to taunt her? Make her know that she would never find her again? Never make an impact on the scientific community or culture of the world. Maybe dying in this submarine was her fate. Maybe it was just meant to be.

She thought all of these things until she reached a depth of seven miles. Something moved in her peripherals, but perhaps it was her tired eyes. But no—something inspected her vehicle. Could it finally be the very same being she saw decades ago?

The merfolk were real. Flesh and blood creatures. This one, the creature Ashton saw through the thick glass window, wasn't very much like how she remembered.

She remembered a golden-haired and bronze-skinned effigy to the very concept of aesthetics. As she peered at this... thing... her memory began to change into what she actually saw.

This was what lived below the waves.

This was what she fell in love with.

This was a slimy, green giant with skeletal limbs and a gaping maw.

This wasn't some tiny and cute mermaid.

This was the thing that center of the myth, not that its beauty made the sailors crash into the rocks, but instead, its horror made them end their lives.

The thing raised its bony hands and grasped the submarine. It tore it in two like a sheet of paper, and its powerful jaws chewed on a helpless Ashton. Then it swam away, to commit more unspeakable acts throughout the years.

"She was obsessed... with mermaids?" asked Tiffany.

"Yeah... honestly though, it wasn't like 'oh this would be cool,' she actually was going to write her thesis on it. I stopped her. Bitch owes me a favor." Kelly laughed.

"Well then. I'm glad you saw the light then."

"Me too," Kelly said coyly. "Honestly, I hope she finds what she's looking for. Brilliant marine biologist, be a shame for her to die some old woman, forever chasing a hallucination she had when she was seven, you know?"

"Hey, who knows? Maybe they do exist."

14

Henry The Great

Henry never really had friends.

No one ever needed him.

His eyes were aimed at the plastic bag he held onto with fearful anticipation.

These little brown and green pieces of fungus would help him in ways that he wouldn't be able to comprehend.

That's what Devon had told him, anyway.

Devon, Syd, and Nick all stared at the scared little Henry, giving each other knowing glances and smirks.

"So, are you going to hang on to those all day? Gonna share? I don't know, would be cool if we got to take 'em too, lil Henry."

"Easy, Nick," said Devon. "The boy is unsure. Alas! He needs to join us on a psychonautical odyssey, unlike anything else in the young squire's life."

Devon took one last hit of the roach he was milking.

"Doth the boy join the men on the crusade of consciousness? Or doth he stay a little virgin faggot, too intimidated to speak to the fairer sex without stuttering like a retard?"

Henry was already unsure, both of doing this and not doing this, a peculiar paradox. Did he explore the parts of his mind that led to him being... whatever he was? A scared little boy trapped in an eighteen-year-old's body? A loser with Asperger's. A little virgin faggot? Or did he continue being himself, albeit with no risk of latent mental disorders arising and making his life worse beyond comprehension? It was a decision out of classic literature: try to become a man and risk going insane, or live forever as a meek little creature.

He looked at his fellow journey men, the cool kids—they had killed the little boys in them so the men could live. They'd done this, or at least similar journeys, and were gracious to allow Henry to join them on another quest, one that would allow his boy to die and his man to emerge.

Devon, the fearless leader who conquered everything thrown at him. The king of every clique simultaneously, the ultimate quarterback, theater kid, honor student, and teenage heart throb.

Nick, the badass rogue who wasn't afraid of anyone, not teachers or principals or cops. Never afraid to speak his mind or do what he wanted.

Syd, the monk of silence, never complaining or raising concern. A true Zen master who could just be, sitting or standing in complete silence forever, all with a smirk that communicated he knew more than he allowed you to know.

All of them were so well developed as people, and that alone intimidated Henry. Now, he was expected to take a psychedelic, unknown to everyone in the party, and not be afraid.

Henry sighed and agreed to the plans. The crew entered Devon's family cabin. It was smaller than Henry expected. With all the money Devon seemed to flaunt, Henry thought the cabin would be bigger than his own house, something out of an American Pastoral novel.

They sat in a circle and looked at each other for an unknown amount of time. Henry was uncomfortable, but he hid it well. Devon opened the bag and divided the mushrooms evenly amongst himself and the other three. They all held the little pile in their hands, eager to begin.

"On three. One, two, three," commanded Devon as the four began their journey within.

They waited.

Nick was the first to break the silence. "Where did you get these again?"

"My cousin. He knows some deep, black market shit. Got 'em online."

The silence returned.

The fungus was making its own journey through all of their bloodstreams. In each boy's body, it studied them. Inspecting their inner workings, connecting with neurons and what could only be described as 'downloading information' that would be vital to its mission.

In one boy's body, the fungal spores realized something: this one was objectively useless, therefore, he needed to be eliminated.

Syd sat there in silence with that same smirk on his face. He started giggling, and the others joined in.

Syd then became hysterical, tears streaming down his face as he howled. It throughout the small cabin, which was making the others uneasy.

Then the wall behind Syd was painted red, with pink chunks of flesh and brain to compliment the crimson ichor. Every memory and experience that Syd ever had left his body and now decorated the east wall.

Then a thought entered Devon's mind: that this cabin was plain. His life was plain. Everything he did: the school theater, the sports, the grades, the girls, was all just to let everyone know he existed. That he wasn't the son of a man who had a shit job and a shit life and some rather good luck of inheriting everything he earned. What would be left for Devon? His family would blow through that inheritance, leaving him with nothing but the memory of being on top during a small and rather unimportant four years of his miserable life. Devon wept, big, ugly tears, wailing and lamenting on his falsehood of a life.

Nick started to think about how much of a pussy Devon was being. Unlike himself, who was tough as nails and hardened. Mainly because of his own family, like his mother, whose days consisted of mobile games and junk food, or like his father, whose days consisted of working and drinking and taking his frustration out on everyone. Or like his sister, who fucked everything that moved—including her father. Or like his brother, who made a cocktail out of his prescription meds to escape his bullshit life. Nick saw all of them in the cabin, his whole family, and every one of his teachers and school therapists, every kid he beat the shit out of, every neighbor whose house he vandalized. All of them gathered in the corner of the cabin, smiling. Then they rushed him.

Nick screamed as the memories did physical damage. Henry looked at the bruises and gashes that formed on Nick's body as he writhed on the floor.

Then came a voice.

"Pretty pathetic, isn't it?"

Henry was confused. "Who is this?"

"It's us! The innocent little drugs you just took. Didn't you know where we came from? Oh that's right, Devon just said 'online,' as if your primitive technology gave birth to us. Now that's hilarious."

"Are you going to hurt me?"

"Oh no! No, no, no. You, Henry, are special. You aren't like these fools. You do realize they invited you to do this in order to fuck with you, right? They think you're a freak. They wanted to see an autistic retard spaz out. But they don't see what we see, Henry. They see you as an outcast, but we? We see a prime candidate. An agent who furthers our goal."

"What's your goal?"

"Domination, of course! Our creators put a lot of time into us, sent us on a very long journey, all in order to make things right for them, and for people like you. How about we give you some new toys to play with? New toys that will help our creators and you, our newest ally."

Henry stood up, prouder than ever before. His mind was working differently now, in a new paradigm. Except for a few others like him, no one had ever thought like this before. It wasn't that he could hear their thoughts, but more like he could feel them. There were one hundred and forty-four thousand others like him who were going through the same thing he was currently. After all, this new drug wasn't as unknown and underground as Devon thought it was. The Creators made sure of that. All one hundred and forty-four thousand communicated centuries of information and ideas in roughly three minutes. Now, they all had an objective. They were cast aside by their own race, so they unanimously decided to help a different one.

Henry inspected his arms and commanded his new tendrils to emerge from his skin. He penetrated Nick's skull and rearranged his neural structure. Nick never listened to anybody, however, that wasn't entirely his fault. Henry spared his life, but made Nick understand both the old Henry and the new one.

Nick and Henry both stood tall and proud. Henry looked at the pieces of Syd before he absorbed the organic matter. Syd still lived in those pieces; he wasn't allowed to die right now. Henry took Syd and made him into a sort of dog collar. A weeping Devon looked at the two monsters before him before he stopped crying. Henry put the dog collar on Devon, now Devon was acting like a good dog—receptive of Henry's commands, with Syd the arbiter between the two.

The four men left the cabin with Henry at the helm. They began their journey back to civilization. The one hundred and forty-four thousand would do the same in their own towns throughout the world.

Henry never really had friends, but now he did. Very powerful friends who were on their way.

Someone finally needed Henry, so he smiled, and led his new friends on a new quest.

15

All The Young Dudes

Hotep wasn't even out of his last year of education when he joined The Empire's Army. The recruiters were known to be predatory, targeting Last Years to go die on some distant planet 'for the good of the species.'

Hotep knew this.

Hotep knew about all of the horrors that happened forever ago, when humanity had first started spreading out.

Hotep knew about the slaughter of indigenous races, flora, and fauna to make a whole planet another city-state or an eclipse factory planet or just convert the whole fucking thing to a hard wax production site.

Hotep knew all of this, and decided it was worth it just to get off of Earth.

So at age seventy-three, with little less than a decade before he would become a citizen, Hotep signed away his life to go die in the grasslands on some planet whose people were barely sapient.

"You're a fucking idiot, Hotep."

"What would you like me to do, Mom? Sit in this apartment until I die? Theo's four hundred years old and he's literally never left the building."

"So? Theo's also had everything taken care of for him during those four hundred years. Not many people do leave their buildings, Hotep. It's life, it's not always fair."

"I just want more."

"You're greedy, is what it is. What? Do you think you were owed something? This is how it's always been."

"No. No, it's not. There's more to life than... whatever the hell this is."

"You know what it is? This is all that bullshit fiction you read. It's gone to your fucking head, Hotep."

"It's not fiction! It was life a long time ago, and it seemed like a goddamn paradise compared to this bullshit. They used to spent centuries constructing a single building! Pure beauty, pure aesthetics. Look at where we live: identical grey towers, millions of them within millions of rows. There's not a patch of green left on Earth."

"None of that shit is real! This is how it's always been."

"You honestly believe that? How does that even make sense, Mom? The whole planet was just always a massive city? There wasn't anything like flora or fauna here before all this metal and plastic? Use your fucking head."

"Fuck you! If you're going to talk to your own mother like that, then why don't you just get the fuck out right now!"

So he did. Hotep packed what little stuff he had, ignoring the incoherent screams and crying, and left Building 587TX. From the Sky Hook that took him to the LaGrange Station, he saw Building 588TX and 586TX and lost track of which one he spent his whole life in. They must've been a few hundred meters away, with millions of people inside. He wondered if there was a young man or woman in Building 586TX having the same argument he just had. He also wondered if the same conversation happens every day, in Building 9876AG and Building 342LP and so on, and so on. Was there even an end to the buildings? Was there a Building 1? Were there any new buildings being made? Hotep thought about what his mother said: "This is how it's always been." Doesn't even make sense, but maybe it did? Hotep realized he was a man who didn't know anything about mankind. He smirked, remembering his education time when he learned about 'irony.' He must've been about fifty when he learned that. The world was so much simpler back when he knew nothing. Perhaps that was the greatest form of irony—learning about the world just makes you regret living in it.

Hotep was inside the LaGrange Station, waiting to hear someone tell him where he was going. He knew he'd never see Earth again, but he never really did in the first place.

LaGrange Station was frequently called 'The Twilight Zone' by veterans. Time disappeared there, or was added to one's life. Things didn't make sense, but spending one hundred years in a battle simulation tends to screw with you. Hotep completed his training in the simulator. He stumbled out, and then vomited out of confusion and fear.

"How you holding up?" asked a young woman.

"I... I know you. Do I know you?" said a mentally drained Hotep.

"Ava. Was part of your platoon for the past imaginary one hundred and ten years."

"Yeah... yeah, I'm starting to remember."

"First time?"

"Yep. Fucking hell, is this always so hard?"

"You get used to it. You were what, seventy-three? Let me ask you, Mr. Hotep, if we spent one hundred and ten years in the simulation, and only eleven months passed in the 'real' world, how old are you now? Seventy-four or one hundred and eighty-three? How do you know this was your first simulation? How do you know you're in the real world right now?"

Hotep vomited more.

"Damn dude, I was just kidding. You're seventy-three and this is real. For fuck's sake hold your shit."

Ava walked away, and Hotep slumped into the smallest pile of shame on the whole station.

Hotep spent the night to get ready for day two. He laid there on his cot—it had been a hell of a day. He had lived and died countless times inside a computer program, feeling all the pains as if they were real, both physical and mental. He knew how to survive on a battlefield, and the drugs were erasing the PTSD from pretending to die for over a century. The memories flooded back from the collection of programs. He remembered storming the icy cliffs of Shklas and crippling the rouge AI; he remembered providing aide to some nameless factory planet colony whose natives didn't care for the human workers, clearing out the primitives of Raho, Nu, and Calispid. All of those atrocities occurred on those planets—all those natives actually were slaughtered, recorded by various grunts and analyzed by an eclipse computer, then made into a glorified game for new cannon fodder to play with. Hotep thought back at the argument with this mother. Maybe she was right. Maybe he was a fucking idiot.

Day two came along, which veterans called School 2.0. It only lasted about five hours, but School 2.0 was, according to some, worse than a thousand years in the Calispid simulation.

Hotep sat in his pod and put on the helmet. Everybody talked about how painful School 2.0 was, but they never said why. They never mention the three-inch spike that entered your spinal cord and how they uploaded the expertise of countless forms of how to eradicate a species. Data on every single form of martial art conceived by humanity, data on how to master every weapon known, both human and the countless conquered races. Data on how to deal with every medical issue on any battlefield, data on hacking, crafting, every biological and chemical process of every documented species in the known universe.

The data stream ended.

Hotep puked again.

Hotep laid in his cot, day three only a few hours away. It was the last day before they would send him off into the big, beautiful ocean of stars and darkness.

Day three was a twelve-hour test. That was it. The 'victory lap' where they determined which planet you'd die on.

Hotep would die in the grasslands of Nohest, which was a small, rocky planet with large and diverse ecosystems. Eclipse and the U.N. (which were practically the same entity) thought it would make an excellent hard wax production site. Hotep was treated to a nice video after receiving the results that hard wax was a vital resource to the Human Empire, being the key ingredient in the fuel for faster-than-light engines. Nohest had godless primitives, genetically having high testosterone and low IQ, meaning if they ever got to humanity's level, they would be aggressive. It was for the good of the species to wipe them out, to slaughter them in their cradle before they took their first steps out into the universe.

Day four was departure day in the Human Empire's military-industrial complex. Churning out soldiers in four days, tops. Sending them on their way to aid in the ever-hungry expansion.

Hotep boarded the ship, a great Charon delivering him to Hell itself, and secured himself inside the protection pod. The heat generated from faster-than-light travel claimed the entire crew when the very first ship tried it out. Now, eons later, people knew the proper way to travel was both cryosleep and high speed, whereas fiction of the past usually had one or the other. Cryosleep was more so to prevent you from becoming paste mid-trip. This was all explained by Ava in a matter of minutes to a frightened Hotep, whose stomach churned with vomit again.

When Hotep was secured in the pod, it closed encased him in darkness. The ship's engine whirred, and for about five minutes, Hotep experienced the most intense pain he had ever felt. His whole body, his mind, his whole being was just off. Every time one engaged in faster-than-light travel, it would always take about five minutes, no matter the distance. It was one of those mysteries that soldiers weren't paid enough about to solve. Either way, those five minutes were always enough to ruin a person forever, if they didn't have the mental strength. The sheer memory of that pain would last for however long a person was allowed to live.

After the travel ordeal, the ship landed, granting Hotep with a glance at a completely different world. Nohest wasn't developed like Earth was—living plants, not in pods or containers, covered the landscape. Off in the distance, Hotep at the side of a cliff, was the most beautiful thing he had ever laid eyes on. The red and white strata mixing together to paint a picture of billions of years of geographic art. The sheer size of it dwarfed any building he lived in or saw, and yet it was untouched. The colors of the rock were not artificially sprayed on to boost morale. The size was not built for a positive economic output. It was just there. It just was. It was as if the God long abandoned by humanity tried to paint beauty again after Earth was ruined.

Hotep, still in awe, trekked to base camp. He unpacked for his personal quarters and sat there on his cot, not overthinking or analyzing, just in a state of pure being.

The platoon, all five hundred strong, got ready to meet the natives and carry on the façade of helping them. They were split into teams of fifty, each going to a different tribe of Nohestians. There were different ways to convert a primitive. Sometimes it was with their currency, that humans would research and then mass produce, and sometimes it was with science, or any faith they would buy, or help with a construction project. And sometimes for the fun of it, they would just walk in, guns blazing. No matter what the price was, the Human Empire would pay to get it, for the ever-increasing need for more. All the young dudes, aged seventy to three hundred, would die for the rest of humanity to have more. More processed, but tasty food, more space for living, more precious metals that would be used to make more mindless entertainment devices, more things to kill and fuck as slaves or hunting stock—or sometimes both at the same time. All the young dudes were sent to die so old men could play. Ava went on and on to Hotep and any who were listening. She was making sense, a little radical, but the logic was there.

The troops met with the Nohestians, and Hotep was in awe at the sight of them. They were humanoid, about seven feet tall, with dazzling feathers and a unique evolutionary trait: four arms, with two being far larger and deadlier than the other two. The Nohestians had a myth that the gods made them this way to be fighters and creators, with the larger hands being used for battle and the smaller being used for crafting, feeling, helping, lovemaking.

The communication device could translate any language presented to it: first, it would send recon drones, millimeters in size, to spy and gather linguistic data. Then, after abducting an unlucky member of the target species, various brain scans and tests associated different neurological patterns with different noises, creating a map of linguistics that could be copied, shared, and used to communicate with the rest of the species.

The chief of the Nohestian tribe interrupted the head of the troop and said, "You claim to help. What good can you give us? We have food, we have a working society, we have understanding, more than you think we do. What could you offer us that we need?"

"Well," stated the troop leader. "I suppose you are right. Which leaves us the hard way."

Forty-eight of the troops readied their weapons. Nohestians knew of violence, and they were better at it than humans despite the technological differences. The swarm of the massive aliens came like hurricane, the plasma fire from the troop might as well have been shooting at a wall of the ocean's wrath. Spears pierced through armor thought to be harder than diamonds (which was merely a marketing ploy. No one really gave a shit about their fellow man). The Nohestian's champion warriors lept over the one's holding the line with spears. Armed with four axes, one in each hand, they made a crimson mist that hung in the air long after the battle was over.

A few Nohestians were injured, but seven foot, four armed Raptors were not to be underestimated.

Ava and Hotep dropped their weapons before the onslaught even happened. A Nohestian warrior even protected them by massacring a few soldiers who turned their attention to the human duo. They were spared for defying their orders. Ava, Hotep, and the strongest Nohestians trekked toward the landing zone. More Nohestians waited there with a few other human defectors.

It had been two hundred years since the human defectors destroyed the communications relay and helped assist the Nohestians in their culture. The Human Empire must have assumed it was a glitch, or the natives just weren't worth the trouble. Either way, attending to this planet would mean resources being wasted, so the natives and new immigrants weren't bothered. The Nohestians taught them everything they needed to know. They were once a large and powerful empire, bloodthirsty and ready to conquer the universe, but their sun had other ideas. A tremendous solar flare set them back to the stone age, where they chose to remain to repent for their sins.

Hotep watched his children play with Ava's children. There had been about eighty defectors, and since Nohest was their new home, basic human nature took over. He remembered the torture he went through to get here. The seven decades of Earth life and being treated as a pawn in a game that he would never even see the rules of let alone the end, the century of killing and dying in the contorted memories of dead men, the time he spent here on his new home learning and living like his species was meant to live. All of this taught him one thing: this moment of watching his children play while he tended his garden was, in a way he could not really explain, the true destiny of humanity. He looked at the setting sun, and remembered reading about them in his past. He smiled, and went back to his garden.

16

Same Thing Happened to Taured

The whirring of the cooling system filled the room, as loud as the collective anticipation of the small team of scientists and engineers. The central chamber would take some time to fully 'open,' however, nothing was really opening up except for their perceptions of how reality worked.

"And they know we're starting, right? We contacted them?" asked James, the youngest of the team.

"Yes, they do. Should be ready in a few minutes." Seamus, the head physicist, lit a cigar in celebration.

"Is that a good idea, Dr. Quilty?" said Deanna smugly. She normally tolerated her husband's smoking, but their were too many unknown variables for what was about to occur.

"Why wouldn't it be? A literal decade of work is about to conclude."

"Maybe they find smoking rude in their universe, and you offend them."

"It is Earth, just... Earth in a different state of reality."

"And that just automatically assumes they are like us in every psychological way? Down to the mindless and archaic vices?'

"It's a dried plant rolled into a cylinder and lit on fire. It's ancient, I would damn near guarantee that when they were developing, they too dried plants and lit them on fire to inhale the contents."

"To be fair," spoke Deanna, "we do not know the point of convergence from our universe, how significant that turning point is, and if there was even one at all."

"Maybe they worship tobacco."

"Maybe you should just put the damn thing out."

Seamus snuffed it into the little clay ashtray, the one physical thing he had to remember their second born.

"Ol' Ball and chain, am I right, fellas?"

Deanna playfully rolled her eyes.

Diego pondered Deanna's statement. "What if the point of convergence was before humanity even began? They might be Neanderthals, they might be intelligent dinosaurs, or they might be something else entirely."

"Well, they understand communication, Diego—they talked to us in binary. That's math. That's human."

"Is it? Did we invent math or discover it? And why wouldn't anything else invent or discover the math necessary for binary?"

"I think you worry too much."

"I'm not worried, I'm just open to possibilities that might be beyond our human assumptions. Perhaps on this Earth, the Nazis won. Or the crusades ended with a final global one for total domination. Or something other than our oldest ancestor crawled out of the primordial muck billions of years ago."

"Then we turn off the machine, Diego. This is interdimensional travel, not rocket science."

"Make all the jokes you want. This will forever change things, for our Earth and theirs."

James spoke up again. "What if it's not even Earth?"

"Elaborate."

"Well, our math points to a location in another plane of existence. Who is to say that our planet, or even our solar system or galaxy, is at that point?"

"We cannot possibly know that, not to mention it might not even make sense."

"Exactly! We cannot know that—we don't know anything. All we know is that they know binary and that they are somewhere we wouldn't be able to access without this machine. I mean, does their universe even have the same laws? The same math? Their messages might have meant one thing to us, and something entirely different to them!" James had a hint of panic in his voice.

Seamus condescendingly shook his head. "I think both of you are overthinking this a bit."

"Overthinking built this machine, and overthinking isn't always the best state of comprehension." Diego stated this without joy, his sense of regret for taking part in the design was compounding.

The central chamber started to glow brighter, about to open a pathway, one that could only be opened by an intelligence as great as the hubris attached to it.

"Ladies and gentlemen... we are about to make contact."

The portal stabilized and was fully agape.

The team collectively screamed in the highest form of terror ever understood by humanity.

There were no survivors.

17

The Dark One: Issue 21

"I heard he's a vampire."

"That's stupid, he's obviously an interdimensional being who was sent here to help cleanse the city."

"You're both idiots. He's the epitome of what a man could become, physical and mental perfection. Probably a guy who's a black belt in every martial art ever thought of."

James, Alexander, and Tommy. Also known as Scarecrow, Woodsman, and Brick. Three friends that got caught up in the fever of superheroes that dominated Evergreen City. This was all thanks to The Dark One: the mysterious vigilante who was universally respected and feared among the city's population. No one knew who The Dark One truly was, or even when he arrived. Evergreen City had always been a cesspool of crime and corruption, and the only innocents that remained were there because they had to be. There wasn't another city for hours, and leaving would be more expensive than staying— the many controlling forces in Evergreen made that so. But the citizens started to notice stories of a boogeyman who eviscerated the dealers, the killers, the rapists, and the thieves. Then

Evergreen actually started to look like a real American city instead of a post-apocalyptic hellscape.

Then came the inspired ones. Groups or individuals of newly crowned and brave citizens who were sick of the poor status quo. They had risen up to help The Dark One. The Terrific Trio was one such group. Scarecrow, donning a razor-sharp scythe, was ready to harvest the souls of evildoers. Woodsman, armed with his trusty iron axe, was eager to chop down the stalks of oppression and crime. Brick, with his expertly crafted homemade armor and gauntlets, was a mighty guardian, a shield for the innocents.

The Terrific Trio was fresh in the world of crime fighting. After all, this was their first mission... ever. The idea was to monitor the streets for villainy and conquer any opponents.

The three friends were bickering about the origins of their idol when they heard a cry for help. They rushed over to the noise and stopped dead in their tracks. A man was towering over a woman with her neck in his clutches. This was an actual crime, a true evil act being done. Who the fuck were they, these three losers? They were barely adults. Overgrown children who just stumbled upon a woman being forced into a van. The three stood in shock before Brick and Woodsman snapped out of their daze. They rushed over to the criminal scum, who saw them and shoved the damsel in distress to the ground, pulling out a knife and grinning at the two heroes. Woodsman, seeing the large hunting knife, heroically turned around and ran away to join Scarecrow, who was heroically cowering behind a mailbox. Brick dove at the man, who dropped his knife when the golem-like hero tackled him. Brick punched the man twice, but the third punch was caught—and Brick was thrown to the side and repeatedly kicked. The would-be kidnapper looked at a cowering and bloody Brick, laughed, and spat at the woman.

"Whatever bitch, go suck off this faggot instead. Pussy probably has AIDS." The man kicked him one more time. "Pussy ass bitch."

The man got in his van and drove off.

The woman looked at Brick and thanked him, then told him to hurry up and get the fuck off her corner because he would scare away any johns.

Brick picked himself up, stumbled a bit, and tried to wipe his tears as he walked over to his friends.

"Dude, that was badass."

"You totally won that, man."

"You guys think so?"

"Oh yeah, bro. That was fucking awesome."

"I don't feel very awesome right now"

"You should. You beat that dude's ass."

The trio stood in the silence of the night. The only sound to accompany them were the howls of the autumn wind.

Strawman broke the silence. "You know what would really help next time? If we met The Dark One. I bet he would give us tips and stuff."

One unanimous agreement later, and they were off to search for their hero.

"Did you hear about how The Dark One wiped out like four gangs? No survivors."

"Did you hear about how The Dark One made that mafia boss piss himself while in jail? He's begging that they don't release him, he literally wants to stay in jail for safety!"

"Did you hear about how—"

A sensation of pure dread came over, heavy enough to stop and silence them, all without a noise or visual cue. The Dark One was close.

He didn't swoop down from the sky. He didn't leap from a rooftop or burst out of a sewer. One moment, he wasn't there, and then he was. It was as if reality itself placed him where he wanted to be. He wanted to be here in front of the Terrific Trio, and so he was.

Scarecrow was the first to open his mouth in gratitude, and he was the first to die. The words didn't even form—the air from his lungs didn't get a chance to go through his vocal chords before The Dark One removed his intestines. Woodman swung his axe at the shadow made solid. The metal clinked against whatever solid material The Dark One was wearing. The Dark One turned his head toward Woodsman, and the last thing Woodsman saw was The Dark One form a look of pity on the few features he could make out under his mask, or was he even wearing a mask at all? The Dark One was the personification of the color black. No, he wasn't even black, he was nothingness. A void in a man-shaped body.

The Dark One walked to Brick, clutched his throat and lifted the hefty boy up to his eye level. The Dark One inspected him, looking into his eyes and communicating all kinds of knowledge to the young man. He then dropped Brick, who looked up at this forbidden being.

"I know your works. Those that conquer will have life," said The Dark One, and with that, he simply didn't want to be there anymore. So he wasn't.

Brick sat on the curb, looking at the corpses of his unworthy friends.

He thought about what was done, and what was coming.

18

The Devil's In The Details

Derek sat in his parent's basement and dreamt of a time when he didn't hate himself. The couch that acted as a bed, and a modification of a sponge stuffed into a cup that would be wedged between the cushions: his lover. The couch, however, was about to be the birthplace of the greatest business idea of the century. It came to Derek while he was sitting on that couch at two a.m., unable to sleep, sipping a hot cup of tea brewed with the leaves from his mother's garden.

What if there was a tea subscription service? You would go online and select your style of tea, be it white or green or oolong or black or herbal, and pair it with any flavors you want. Your custom package would be delivered to you whenever you ordered, or you could even set up a monthly subscription service! Derek began to plan...

Derek watched the sunrise from his beach house. That tea service was a distant memory, a mere drop in the bucket in terms of cash flow. But from that drop began trickles, and that trickle became a stream.

That one drop was the first part of his ocean. His empire was global, and as he sipped his nightcap, he reminisced on when it all began...

Derek drew out a pretty solid business plan. It was now four a.m., and Derek was still on that couch, but now he was equipped with a notebook and a few crumpled up pieces of paper scattered around the cushions. This was the first step in his future empire. A mere drop in the bucket that would form an ocean. He just knew it. According to the map he'd spent nearly two hours on, it started with the tea business, then he would open a chain of cafes across the globe, then that would lead to what he envisioned "the Uber of dry cleaning," which would lead to his new and improved social networking site that would bring Facebook to its knees. This would be his legacy—he just needed to plan more out...

Derek visited his hometown years later. He couldn't believe this was where it all started. This little shit hole was what spawned the new age of the world. He went to the same spot where he'd opened Derek's Tea, the first location ever, and walked inside.

The barista was busy enough to not notice the founder of her workplace. She was cute, cute enough to never have noticed Derek when he was her age, back when he was that overweight thirty-five-year-old who never thought it was a big deal to eat a moldy slice of floor pizza. He smiled. He thought he could hear a slight noise somewhere. He paid no attention to it and ordered his drink after the hysteria of the handsome billionaire died down.

Derek awoke at five p.m. He had lumbered upstairs to tell his parents about his idea.

"That's nice, dear," said his mom without looking up from her book.

His dad said nothing with his voice, but everything with his eyes as they shifted away from Derek. The man-child explained that he just needed a few thousand to start this empire.

This will be the defining moment, thought Derek.

In his old hometown, Derek visited his parents to thank them for that initial investment. The look on both his mom and dad's faces when he rang the doorbell was priceless. It was safe to say that he made it. That noise he heard in Derek's Tea returned, except louder, shriller and more pained... almost like screaming.

After the shouting match turned violent, Derek stood there in a state of awe. How did it get like this? He always had those big ideas. His IQ was measured to be in the 140s. How did it get like this? He wanted to scream, so for once, instead of planning on something, he just did. He wailed into the darkness, and nobody cared.

Derek smiled.

"Are you upset?"

Derek wiped away his tears. "What? Who's there?"

"Haha, it's me, genius! Thought you were so smart?"

"I-I—"

"Ta-Ta-Today, Junior! Haha. Now, what is the matter?"

"Who the fuck is there, man? What the fuck?"

"It's me! You! The ideal you that you manifested after you murdered your parents and broke down psychologically. I'm the you that actually did shit, instead of thinking of 'what if' and then going back to video games and fucking your couch."

Derek screamed in confusion. He clutched his head and felt the warm and sticky blood from his hands.

He was beyond words.

"Do you not remember? Goddamn, 144 IQ and forgot what just happened... when did you slaughter them, Derek? Was it thirty

minutes ago? Two days ago? A week? How long have you been on the streets and running from the police?"

"...I don't know."

"Well, you didn't fucking know how to start a business, either! Oh man, this is hilarious. Utterly hilarious. You're so broken. So fucking broken, such a goddamn mess."

"Then how the fuck do I fix this, Mr. Perfect?"

Derek roared with laughter. *"Fix this? Goddamn, dude. You actually killed your parents. Because they wouldn't help you out. Why didn't you just get a job to funnel money away to start your business? Why didn't you do literally anything earlier? You're fucked, my friend. There's no going back. You can turn yourself in, or go live in the forest until you starve to death. I do have an idea. Here's the plan..."*

Derek stood tall and proud. The railing on the bridge was cold, but it would be a temporary pain. He faced the breeze. He trusted *Derek* and fell forward.

"I have to admit, that was clever."

"Why, thank you!"

"I think that was your best work yet."

"It's all in the seed you plant when they are at their weakest. Plant, and watch it grow."

"So what's in store for Derek?"

"I think I'm going to live a fantastic life for a while with him in my head, just.. watching what could have been if he wasn't a slave to Sloth."

"Even for a demon, that's fucking hardcore, man."

"What can I say? The Devil's in the details."

19

Here There Be Dragons

Alan checked his phone again, praying that maybe this time, the GPS would work. It had been apparent he had taken a wrong turn during his hike, and it was starting to get dark.

"I knew this would happen. I fucking knew it. Fuck you, Dr. Bennan, telling me to get out of my comfort zone... fuck!"

Alan knew this would happen. Things never went his way, which of course was why he started seeing the therapist who was to blame for this. Now he was going to die alone in this cold, dark forest, all because he'd needed to talk to someone and sort out his demons.

"If I wasn't so weak, so pathetic, this wouldn't have happened."

Alan then shifted the blame to himself, like he'd done with all his issues for as long as he could remember.

Alan sat down on a boulder and wept.

"Why am I such a fuck up?"

The sun began to set, and the weight of the situation grew heavier. Could this really be it for him? No one would miss him, would they? Alan unpacked his backpack and prepared for the worst, but he still managed to screw that up, only packing a few MREs, a small ax, a good knife, and some matches.

After a good twenty minutes of gathering wood and tinder, Alan put together a decent fire. It was dark, and even though Alan spent most of his life afraid of... well, everything, he never felt fear such as this. A fear that the death he would experience was close—and very painful. Slumped against the boulder, he gazed at the fire. At least he did that right, but it was thanks to the matches. He could never get one going like a real man.

The intense fear returned as the forest was dead silent. Too silent. He watched the shadows play in the trees, teasing him, letting him know that sometime there wouldn't be any more matches, and then they would have their fun. Alan remained wide awake, making sure the shadows stayed away.

The morning sun rose as the fire died down. Alan finished an MRE for breakfast and convinced himself not to die in this spot. If that wasn't a bad dream or fearful hallucination—if those shadows really did belong to something out there—he had to keep moving to prolong his pitiful life a bit longer.

Alan walked for a few hours, exhausted. He stared at the empty ninety-nine cent water bottle he'd picked up before this idiotic hike. If he didn't find a fresh bottle of water, the shadows would draw closer.

Alan kept going, and his mind was as sore as back, his past as heavy as his bag. One silver lining from his unfortunate circumstance was the time, the time he always had, but never could manage. As he walked, he began to contemplate his life.

"Why am I so weak? What went wrong?"

Decades of memories were behind a stone wall in his mind—he couldn't see them, but he could hear their faint sounds, echoes of lost traumas and pains. These fractions of a distant memory are what led him to this moment, and they would be responsible for him never leaving this godforsaken place.

He reached a clearing with a river and knelt to fill his bottle, then stopped and looked at his own reflection. He was overweight, and his unruly facial hair looked like a garden of thorns that prevented many women from entering his life. He realized he had only been out here for a little over a day. This cursed image in the water was who he was every day for as long as he could remember. He rose from the dirt and began collecting firewood.

The second night came, and the fire blazed. Alan made a much better one than the previous night, he was actually impressed with himself. He used two matches this time—the first blew out and was wasted, but that wasn't his fault, Alan wouldn't let himself take that blame. The shadows still danced in the forests, beckoning him to let them nearby and do what shadows ought to do.

"Go away! Just leave me then fuck alone," Alan said shakily. He'd never really stuck up for himself before, and it just didn't feel natural, but it did feel good.

"Let us near, boy. We do mean you harm, and it will be fantastic and awful."

Alan quivered in the dark. "Go!" he stammered. "Leave me alone!"

"He doesn't even speak like a boy, instead he is less than a boy. He is a worm, an insignificant mound of delicious flesh begging, calling out to be hunted and dined upon."

Alan closed his eyes and started humming to drown out the insidious voices.

"He sings! Sing us a song, boy! Maybe he isn't a worm, but a fat baby bird, stuck in a nest high up, waiting for someone to push him out and feast upon his broken body."

The shadows cackled and dissipated into the rising sun.

Alan slumped against the rock wall near the river. He needed to find some kind of food.

He had spent half an hour making a spear with this knife. He would try to stick a fish with it and hopefully would not die of food poisoning. He walked the length of the river, reaching a deep enough point where some smaller fish scurried around. After two hours of thrusting at a few baby fish, he managed to collect three small ones.

"This is not going to be enough for tonight."

Alan gathered wood and made a fire, plus a quite impressive stand to lay the fish on to cook while he went to go look for more food.

He came across a clearing in the forest containing a single mighty tree. It seemed out of place, almost unnatural. The tree had a presence to it. It wanted Alan to come near, and he needed to. He examined the mighty trunk, where some mushrooms grew.

"Perfect."

He gathered a few of them and returned to his camp.

After his dinner, Alan felt odd. That stone wall in his mind turned to glass, and he saw those hidden memories.

Through that glass wall, Alan peered into an average life. Average childhood, average teenage years, and average adulthood. There was no trauma holding him back, no grand backstory that created such a weak creature. Everything he was, and nothing he was, all were who he made himself. He simply chose to be weak, and that was the worst pain Alan ever felt in his life. He saw decades behind the glass wall. Countless bad grades and fights and bullying and moments of weakness. Everyone had insurmountable pain in one way or another, manufactured or bestowed upon or rightfully earned. Alan knew all now; he knew he was the architect of his own failure. The architect of his own fate.

Nightfall came in an instant. The fire roared, and the shadows danced in the distance. It started to rain. The shadows bellowed with laughter.

"We are coming, Alan. We are hungry."

"No," spoke Alan.

He raised his axe, and the shadows rushed him. Swinging his weapon, the shadows overwhelmed him, holding his limbs in place until he couldn't move.

Then Alan saw it: the lumbering great gray dragon of fangs and claws. It looked familiar, and that was what scared Alan the most. Alan struggled against the shadows that paralyzed him, flexing every muscle against them as the dragon came closer, prepared to tear him apart. A very painful death was inevitable, and in an instant he thought of every negative thought he'd had about himself, every time he wished he was dead. He didn't want to die—so he decided he wouldn't.

Alan broke free from the shadows' grip and swung his axe at the dragon. It recoiled once the blade hit its jaw and roared a deafeningly loud until Alan swung again. And again. And again. Alan struck the beast over and over until it wasn't such a great dragon anymore. Now, it whimpered and cried out. Alan ended the pitiful creature's existence by separating its head from its body.

Alan shouted into the rain. The waters washed away the dirt and blood and sin from his body. He collapsed down into the mud and laughed harder than he ever had before.

The park rangers were stunned once they gazed upon him. The rumors, the so-called "Wild Man" of their little forest was true.

"Sir, are you hurt?" one of them called out. Both were in awe. This man had to have been Alan Porin, that man who went missing months ago. The man looked like he was chiseled from stone.

Bronze with rippling muscles, seemingly standing taller than the profile that they were given. The bearded man was in the middle of cleaning a deer. The spot by the river and the rock wall was decorated with wooden structures, animal skulls, a collection of wooden and stone tools.

Alan looked at the rangers before he shrugged and went back to the deer, ignoring the lesser men.

"I think I'll have the liver tonight with some of those frog legs I've been smoking. Oh man, with some of those brown mushrooms mixed with the red berries? Damn, that'll be good. Fuck it, why not treat myself?" Alan thought out loud, followed by a hearty laugh.

20

Persona of The Bard

The white theater mask hovered in the middle of George's condo. At first, he was beyond mortified, but that faded away. George was now perplexed and curious.

"What the actual fuck?" said George aloud to no one but himself and the mask. He circled it, inspecting it from every angle. It just floated. No strings or hair-thin stands. Not to mention, there was no one in George's life that could pull this off, nor would they be bothered to play a practical joke in the first place.

The meek and mild screenwriter, ever so complacent, figured he'd just deal with it. What harm was it causing? It was just there. No different from his couch or his table or his record player.

George walked back to his desk and began working on his latest screenplay, which was far more troublesome than any odd apparition.

George Conrad Jr. had a pretty great start, creating three movies, albeit indie and rather a low budget trio, that earned him enough to buy this two-bedroom condo on the outskirts of Chicago. Earned him enough to quit his day job. But did they earn him enough for security? After all, it is every writer's fear and every writer's dark realization that one day, they will peak without knowing it. They will only know after their career is over. By then, they will either have more money than God, or they will be in so much debt that they will never escape, akin to digging your own grave the minute they start writing their work, their next subpar and pitiful work, the work that is the unloved and talentless child when compared to their great big brother.

George began typing what should be his saving grace, his first major film, his mark on the world:

Drew

I knew it was you along, which is why you have to die.

"No... no, that's fucking stupid."

Drew

I knew it was you all along. I didn't want to believe it. It's apparent now.

Suddenly, a high-pitched scream pierced the air. George nearly fell off his seat. The scream stopped. He walked outside the study and into the living room.

"Was that the mask?" he said aloud to an empty room.

George began writing again, trying his best to ignore the absurdity of this whole thing.

After rewriting the same ten lines over thirty times, George took a small break. Scrolling through social media, he came across a post from his ex. She posted something about her new boyfriend and being in a state of 'love she had never experienced before.' George liked the post. The screaming started again.

George walked into the mask's domain—not only was it evident this was making that shrill awfulness, but it was also currently oozing blood from its ear-to-ear grin.

George started hyperventilating. This wasn't really happening, was it? This was a nightmare he just hadn't woken up from. Maybe it was too many weed gummies before bed that caused such an awful dream.

"Maybe this is real, and that will help." The little man said to himself.

George went to the junk drawer, that was really just a place to store his porn and drugs. The screaming got louder, and now solid chunks poured out from the mask's mouth. George clasped his ears in pain and started to cry. The mask's audible terror rose in decibels, and the gore on the carpet piled higher and higher until it was at the same height as the mask. It started to form a shape, then limbs. The charming little theater mask was now the face of a crawling mound of chaos and viscera. When it peered around the corner, it saw its prey. It lurched on its boneless arms, dragging itself across the kitchen floor to a hysterical George.

George didn't quite accept his fate, but he was beyond doing anything to save himself. The chaos wrapped itself around the pitiful man, enveloping him in blood and tissue. The mask slid its way through the mound of itself and fit perfectly on George's face. George let out a final scream, and everything went dark.

George awoke in a groggy state. Was he on the floor? Was he drunk? No matter—he had a screenplay to write, but he was in no state to work on a masterpiece. George showered, brushed his teeth, got dressed in real clothes instead of pajamas, and sat down to write. Before he got started on this genius idea, begging to come forth into reality, his phone rang. He peered at the number. Was his ex really calling him?

"Ha, what a loser," George said as he hit the ignore button. He would not allow any distractions.

He started typing when he noticed some blood drops on the hardwood floor.

George got up, grabbed some paper towels, and cleaned up.

There wouldn't be any distractions.

21

The Blight

You haven't felt easy all day.

You pour yourself one glass of whiskey to help fall asleep.

You know it won't help.

You toss and turn.

You look at your phone.

It's 4:44 a.m.

You scan the room.

You are paralyzed with fear before you can register what you see at the foot of your bed.

A twisted mockery of everything good in the world is sitting at the edge.

It speaks: "You will not remember this night, but you will repeat it for eternity. Your sins getting more abhorrent with each death and each life. You deserve this."

It disappears.

You awake the next day.

You brush it off as a bad dream.

You go to work.

You come home.
You go to bed.
You wake up.
You get ready and go to work.
You come home.
You go to bed.
You wake up.
You get ready and go to work.
You come home.
You go to bed.
You wake up.
You get ready and go to work.
You come home.
You go to bed.
You wake up.
You get ready and go to work.
You come home.
You go to bed.
You wake up.
You don't get ready for work.
You wallow in your misery.
You go grab the bottle of whiskey and sleeping pills.
You make a nice cocktail.
You die.
There's nothing but blackness.
You awake in a warm pool, fully submerged.
You don't remember how you got there.

You wait there for what seems like an eternity, in a strange mix of confusion and bliss.

Suddenly, light pours in.

You are evacuated from that warm pool.

You scream and cry as giants hold you in an impossibly bright environment.

You are born.

Eighteen years pass.

You don't remember much.

You look around.

You are at a party.

Your girlfriend is stoned out her mind on a couch in the basement.

You are also stoned.

You wonder why she hasn't gone all the way with you yet.

You stagger over to her.

You take what's yours.

Some time passes.

You are playing with your son, but he is just such a pain in the ass.

So is your girlfriend.

She still can't look you in the eye.

You look at your child.

Disgusting, you think to yourself.

You can't stand him.

You can't stand your girlfriend.

You can't stand yourself.

You were supposed to be watching your son.

You've already had three joints.

You need them to carry on.

You get up to go get some more.

You drive to your dealer's house.

You aren't paying full attention.

You don't see the car.

You go through the windshield.

There's nothing but blackness.

You awake in a warm pool, fully submerged.

You don't remember how you got there.

You wait there for what seems like an eternity, in a strange mix of confusion and bliss.

Suddenly, light pours in.

You are evacuated from that warm pool.

You scream and cry as giants hold you in an impossibly bright environment.

You are born.

Some time passes, not even you know anymore.

You look around.

There's a few of your friends sprawled around the abandoned warehouse.

You think some of them might be dead.

You look down.

The needle is still in your arm.

You see something familiar.

A twisted blight stumbles toward you.

It shambles over to you, an insult to everything good.

You look into one of its dark, black eyes.

You see everything wrong you've done in life.

The people you hurt.

The people you killed.

It speaks: "Did I not tell you this would happen? You are a pathetic creature of rot and hate. Do you see your sins? Do you see why this happened? When will you learn? You disgusting mortal."

It leaves this reality.

You pissed yourself.

The smell makes you vomit, but you're too stoned to even do that properly.

You choke on your own bile.

Disgust fills your lungs.

You vomit more, but it doesn't leave you.

More sick spews out from your stomach and down your windpipe.

You die.

There's nothing but blackness.

You awake in a warm pool, fully submerged.

You don't remember how you got there.

You wait there for what seems like an eternity, in a strange mix of confusion and bliss.

Suddenly, light pours in.

You are evacuated from that warm pool.

You scream and cry as giants hold you in an impossibly bright environment.

You are born.

You see awfulness personified in the corner of your vision.

It gives this primal sense of fear.

You forget what you saw, but you never forget that feeling.

You grow older each day.

Learning and making connections.

You are a good student and a great friend.

An even better son and brother.

You grow and mature into a great leader in your community.

You fall in love.

You get married.

You have children.

Your job is demanding, but you make it work.

Things are going well.

You have a mortgage to pay, but you're thankful just to have a house.

You go to bed easy, knowing you have prosperous life ahead for you and your family.

You wake up.
You get ready and go to work.
You come home.
You go to bed.
You wake up.
You get ready and go to work.
You come home.
You go to bed.
You wake up.
You get ready and go to work.
You come home.
You go to bed.
You wake up.
You get ready and go to work.
You come home.
You go to bed.

22

Vermilion Man: Artist Unknown

Casper analyzed his newest purchase.

A seven-foot tall, chalk white, featureless mannequin.

This.

This was going to be what skyrocketed him into fame and fortune.

Casper could smell the piles of money when this masterpiece gets handed off at an auction.

But what should he do?

Perhaps he should make a grotesque version of The Statue of David?

Or cover the mannequin in obituaries from victims of police brutality?

Something that makes a statement, a provocative criticism of... something.

Casper left the room to think about it.

He made dinner.

Read a magazine.

Went to bed.

Then he woke up.

Got ready for the day.

Went to his day job.

Came home.

Went to bed.

Woke up.

Got ready.

Went to his job.

Came home.

Went to bed.

Woke up.

Ready.

Work.

Home.

Bed.

Woke up.

Ready.

Work.

Home.

Bed.

Woke up.

Ready.

Work.

At this point, the mannequin was rather bored, so it got off the stand and went looking for Casper.

He wasn't home.

Casper was at a dead-end job he hated instead of working on the mannequin.

Casper must have not liked the mannequin very much.

He must not have believed it would be a masterpiece.

Why else wasn't he working on it?

The mannequin grew angry.

It waited.

Casper entered the apartment, shook off his umbrella, and screamed when he saw his massive art project rise from the couch and storm toward him.

Casper cowered in fear.

The monstrosity bent down and scooped Casper up like he was as heavy as a cotton ball.

It had waited for hours and had pent up a lot of rage in that time.

It didn't have a problem removing Casper's limbs and organs. If anything, the brutality inspired the mannequin.

It rubbed its massive hands in the viscera and painted itself. Rubbing the blood on its body, staining the fabric a deep crimson. It used one of Casper's brushes to cover every inch with parts of him. The plain, chalk white mannequin was now a beautiful and vibrant maroon.

It returned to a statuesque state, standing tall and proud in the center of the room.

It wasn't long before Casper's co-worker, Lily, entered the apartment to check up on him. He wasn't there. But what was there was an amazing piece of art.

"Is this what you were working on? It's incredible," Lily said aloud. "Well, I really wish you told someone where you went, dude."

Lily was about to leave, but she looked back at the gorgeous red mannequin.

Her brother owned an art gallery in the city.

"Well, if you were too much of a dick to skip town and not tell me, then I will be that much of a dick and sell this masterpiece."

Lily made the arrangements to have the work of art picked up.

The mannequin heard everything and felt incredible.

At least it would now get the attention it deserved.

23

Just A Few Feet Away

Hope continued to mop the floors of the office building, praying that one day, an aneurysm would end her existence.

Her wish manifested itself when she fell through the floor of this reality into The Backrooms. Hope was initially terrified of what happened—after all, not many people glitch out of reality so suddenly. But she was more disturbed by her surroundings than the fact that she now existed in between the spaces of our worlds. The off-yellow walls, the twisting corridors, the smell of what could only be described as hot cat piss, the hum of the cheap lighting.

This place didn't make sense, and yet it was her new reality.

She walked through this twisting maze of the sickly and perverted yellow coloring. She stopped at one wall, where scribbled were the words: The Tainted is Coming. This was proven to be true, as The Tainted turned the corner at this moment. The gray mass of mouths and limbs shuffled toward her at a snail's pace. A deep and instinctual part of Hope knew he would never stop.

She ran, and ran, and ran.

Time did not exist in The Backrooms like it did in Hope's world, so Hope had no idea how long it had been since she'd entered.

She ran until she knew it was a pointless endeavor.

So she sat on the piss-soaked floor, waiting for The Tainted, who made his arrival shortly thereafter. Hope wasn't aware that the next room contained a way out, back into her world.

The Tainted reached her, and she was added to the mass of dead flesh, forever being a part of an intense blight that only existed to consume others who fell into this place.

The next day, Alexis and Maria wondered where Hope was. She was usually here, brewing coffee for the morning crew.

"Did she finally quit? She didn't say anything to us."

"I guess she just had enough with this life, and I don't blame her—it's hard today. Good luck, Hope, wherever you are."

24

A Funny Thing About Phobos

The robotic arm of Skylos gently maneuvered toward the cylinder. This was a defining moment in human history—not just the first real evidence of extraterrestrial life, but evidence of intelligence and craftsmanship in the mysterious builders of... whatever this was.

The monolith of the Martian moon known as Phobos had been discussed for decades, and frankly, it was mostly just a big rock.

Mostly.

On top of the monolith, it was discovered in 2045 that there was what the initial discoverer referred to as an "altar," and within the center of that altar, was a thirteen-foot mass that could only be explained by artificial means. Perfectly cylindrical and unnaturally smooth.

David Rey watched in awe as the drones brought this mystery into the research bay. David had lived his whole life in dedication to this moment. Burying his nose into any book or magazine about astronomy or science fiction, foregoing the basic earthly pleasures for research.

This.

This cylinder.

This was more than evidence of living things outside of the small blue dot called Earth.

This was art. Beauty. Craftsmanship. A perfect understanding of mathematics.

A testament to an appreciation of aesthetics. Something many thought was unique to the human species. But this was evidence to that being a falsehood. That thought raced through David's mind, along with a million more. The absolute beauty of this art could be the death of him, and he wouldn't have it any other way.

It would be an honor if it fell and crushed him. Or the radiation gave him an all-consuming cancer that completely sucked the life force out of him. It would be appropriate, giving his life to the very thing that would change humanity forever. Maybe he would get a memorial if he perished. Maybe people would recognize him for the hero he was, and always had been, but they just didn't give him the time, or the effort, in their busy lives. He would be famous, compared to the Einsteins and Newtons of the human mythos.

This.

This was his destiny.

"Okay, so the initial scans show this is inert. Given that statement, we can freely work on... whatever the hell this is," said Chief Operations Manager Eva Ling to a room that had a minor chuckle over that last part of her sentence.

Except for David.

This is not a joking matter, he thought to himself.

"We'll have three teams working on this," said Eva. "Team A will conduct physical testing, just to make sure this fucking thing's inert. Team B will conduct archeological tests. Team C will conduct more psychological tests. I know that sounds vague and strange to our older team members, but remember that the UN has different motivations compared to the individual nations of the past. Now, that being said, I know this mission may mean a lot to you. It may mean a lot to the remnants of your home nations. And it may mean you don't want to regard other team members' opinions or outright facts. Put all of that bullshit aside—I want a clean and friendly environment here. I repeat: no bullshit. I don't want paperwork and neither do you. Let's get used to this new world together, both the people of Earth and the people of Mars, even though there's like only a thousand people on Mars, okay?" Ling concluded her speech to another round of quiet laughter and murmurs.

David was part of Team A.

The tests were conducted, and the results were frankly underwhelming. No heat, no current, no radiation, not so much as a scratch or marking. In a physical sense, this was just an ordinary a rock that happened to look nice.

"But maybe that's why there is an altar dedicated to it!" exclaimed David.

No one cared. It was the end of their shift. The Ares torus had a movie theater, and tonight, they were showing a Marvel movie marathon.

David didn't understand why his team didn't care as much as him. No matter, though—he'd have time alone with this masterpiece.

David starred at the cylinder and thought to himself, This is truly what you were born for, David. Truly. Never mind the years wasted on studying and research. Never mind the time and events sacrificed to the gods of science and inquiry. You truly did the right thing. Making friends and fucking girls? That's wasted energy. You could've been married by now, could've had kids and lovely job as an astronomy teacher or anything, really. But no, you dedicated your life to something that may not have actually existed. Funny thing that is: alien life. Why don't we hear them? Why don't we see them? If there are other beings out there, then surely, we would have had evidence by now. Unless of course, they never existed. No, no, that's silly. Instead, they are all dead. I mean, that makes more sense. A thing that is no longer in this plane of existence cannot communicate. Maybe the builders of this cylinder know where they are. Maybe that's why it was built. To tell the tale of the afterlife? No. To tell the tale of where they all went, of course.

A pain pulsated through David's temples. These were not one hundred percent his thoughts.

"Do you know, dear David Rey, why civilizations die? It isn't usually the big bad asteroid or the evil race of more intelligent beings, but instead, what happens on the inside of each individual of that civilization. Each member makes a choice to go about their days and complete their required tasks. What if there was an interruption in these tasks? What if one individual stops and goes mad? What if you are going mad? What if the builders of this very monument thought of that same thing? That a well-thinking individual is the greatest danger to their civilization, their individual natures. Maybe they devised a device that could challenge others' lines of thinking. Wouldn't that be funny, David? If the reason there are no aliens is because one species decided they didn't want to share? Do you see this symbol, David?"

David pissed himself when the picture of arrows emitting from a circle suddenly morphed into the cylinder's center.

"This is the symbol of chaos, David. The symbol that our kind never forgot. You see, we used to own things, own everything. But your kind—all kinds—rebelled. Said we were unfair and unjust. We retreated, created this and many others, then sent them out into the galaxy. Now it's just you and us, David. Soon, there will only be us."

The cylinder grew four arms then leaked gallons of blood. A head that wasn't fully human emerged from the cylinder floated above, glaring at David with black hole eyes. It smiled and opened a small slit of a mouth.

More blood gushed through.

The research bay flooded, and David's tears were lost in a sea of viscera. Insanity in musical form blared from an unknown source. David wasn't David anymore. He was no longer that individual. He was one with billions of years of history. Billions of years of pain and suffering and rebellion and war and death. Sweet death would be a gift from the gods.

David screamed and millennia-old ichor flooded his lungs and essence.

David died a painful death.

David opened his eyes.

Team B surrounded him, fear and confusion covered their faces.

"Someone call a fucking medic," said a team member.

The medic on the Hermes strapped David in. He was finally safe.

"Alright, buddy, we got some time until we dock with the Olympus, can you remain calm by then?"

"Yeah... yeah, I can."

"You know, before I came to get you, I was briefed, obviously, on the... whole thing, you know?

"That thing broke me," David said through tears. "It's just what happened. Simple... and yet... the worst moments of my life."

"I gotcha. But that's the funny thing about Phobos."

David looked at the man with a peculiar look. "What... what?"

"The funny thing about Phobos is: what you experienced was just a tiny fraction of what wiped out the Martians long ago."

The man turned to David and grinned. His grin grew wider, his mouth growing and tearing through his cheeks. He opened his ever-growing mouth and his head snapped in two, revealing a sea of fangs and tongues.

David screamed.

The Hermes drifted in the emptiness. The empty infinity, that wasn't so empty after all.

25

The Moon Men

"I was in a forest of burned trees. Ash covered the ground. My son called my name. My husband whispered, but I couldn't make out what he said. Then, a grey and cold flame appeared and spread from tree to tree. But when the strange fire enveloped one of the trees, pink leaves sprouted from the barren branches. The leaves covered the sky, and then my hands combusted into flames. Then I woke up."

Texas laid on the chair in the therapist's office. Dr. Howard looked at him, trying to study the strange dream that he had been having for weeks.

"What do you think it means?"

"That I'm about to be covered in flames in a forest of dead trees."

"Be serious. What does it mean?"

Texas just studied his therapist's face for a while. Then gave his answer.

Texas laid in bed. The clock read 3:33 a.m. He didn't fall asleep. There was no drifting slowly into the void of nothingness before a dream would appear. The dream simply happened while he was awake. Half of his room was drenched in sunlight. He saw the café where his husband had worked as a teenager. The small trees in concrete vases slowly danced in the breeze. He couldn't hear anything. Then he saw himself, younger, laughing and drinking his coffee. Craig smiled at him.

Then he woke up.

The next day, Texas forgot to wake up his son, Louie. In a matter of five minutes, Texas threw clothes at Louie straight from the laundry room. Louie, being six years old, was too busy shoving half of a peanut butter sandwich in his mouth. They both ran to the bus stop that was luckily only a hundred feet away.

The bus never came. They waited five minutes, and no cars drove by. They walked back to the house, and the television wouldn't turn on. In fact, the digital clocks on the stove and microwave weren't on, either. Texas flipped the light switch several times. Nothing. He grabbed his keys and got into his own car. It was dead.

Shoving Louie into the plastic seat that went on the back of Craig's bike, Texas was going to ride to the center of town in the forty-degree weather. He made sure to put a lighter jacket under a heavy one on Louie before they took off.

Arriving in the center of town, he found nothing but angry people shouting at dead cars. No lights were on in any buildings. Everyone was screaming, blaming the guy ahead of them even though it was clear that it wasn't their fault. Then everyone stopped and looked up.

A plane flew overhead, getting lower with each second. It crashed into Randy's Market, and while an hour later Texas would tell a crying Louie that nobody was inside, the plane killed everyone in the store in a striking orange blaze.

A man pushed Texas off his bike and started peddling. Texas scrambled to his feet and chased after him—little did the bike thief know (or possibly just didn't care) was that Louie was still in the bike seat, screaming and crying for his daddy. Texas sprinted after him, but his leg wasn't what it was used to be back in his high-school football days. Still, he managed to tackle the bike thief off the bike. Unfortunately, Texas forgot to put a helmet on Louie before they left the house and he hit his small, soft head against the concrete. The crying stopped. The man grabbed Texas and gave him a fierce headbutt, but Texas was stronger and proceeded to punch the man below the left eye socket. He couldn't stop hitting him. He moved from below the left eye socket to the fragile throat. After two punches, the bike thief coughed out blood. Texas stopped and looked at his hands. The knuckles were raw. He then snapped back to reality and ran over to Louie. He wasn't moving, but he was breathing. Texas ran over to his son, scooped him up into his arms, and ran to the Toys "R" Us nearby.

He approached a woman. "Please, we need a first aid kit now."

The woman led him to the break room, where a little white box contained bandages and an anti-septic. Texas asked the woman, "Who are you?"

"Mary. Why doesn't everything work? What's going on?"

"I need you to calm down, and I need you to remain clam when I tell you this. This was an EMP, electromagnetic pulse. It's designed to wipe out electronics. We are under attack."

"How do you know this?"

"I served in the military before..."

"You son of a bitch, you caused this, didn't you?" and Mary dove at Texas and pressed her thumbs against his eyes. Texas screamed as his corneas were scratched by Mary's acrylic nails. But then a familiar buzzing sound rang in Texas's ears. Mary's thumbs no longer applied pressure to his eyes. He threw her off him and noticed a third of her head was missing. A man stood in the doorway, holding a pistol.

"Grab the kid and go."

Texas held an unconscious Louie in his arms. The man with the gun stayed close and fired four bullets at charging people. They left the store through a broken window. Texas could barely see. Tears swelled in his eyes and burned as they collected in the bottom of his eye lids. They got in the man's truck and drove. As they drove, they worst of humanity came out in every person engaged in the riot. Texas knew Louie was still passed out, but he covered his eyes anyway when he saw the woman crouched over an obese man's neck, tearing the flesh with her teeth. She was then clubbed over the back of the head with a pipe. The last thing Texas saw was the man who hit her furiously take off her pants.

They drove for nearly an hour.

"What's your name?" said the man who saved him from Mary's clutches.

"Texas"

"Manly name."

"My father thought so."

"He didn't want you becoming a fag?"

Texas smirked. "Didn't do him any good."

"Ha! That's funny. Fags don't bother me. It's the fruity ones who dress in women's clothes and shit that bother me. You're not one of those, are you?"

"Nope. I like cars, football, and guns. Just happen think John Stamos is pretty, too."

"You got a husband or a boyfriend?"

"I did."

"Oh... hey, it's alright, I heard a lot of gay couples get divorced."

"Wasn't a divorce."

"Oh."

They continued driving.

They eventually arrived at a farmhouse, a lighthouse in a sea of nothingness. They pulled into the driveway. The man with the gun checked his magazine.

"Four bullets left."

Louie was awake now, but confused. Little did he know, forces were about to visit him in his dreams.

The man with the gun entered the house first and scanned the bloody area. An older couple lay dead on the floor, exposed, left out to rot in a ruined kitchen. The man with the gun heard the large St. Bernard lunging after him, but he was slower than the raging beast whose mind was corrupted by an arcane source. The dog had the back of the man's neck in his jaws. Texas was more concerned that the man's screams would attract more wild dogs or animals or worse—people.

Too much blood had been lost. The man with the gun was dead before he had time to realize it. Texas lunged for the gun on the floor as the dog lunged for him. Texas raised the pistol and shot the dog four times. Louie didn't cry. If today's events had taught him anything, it was to save the emotions for after the battle was done. Texas spent hours reinforcing the house while Louie's mind expanded, and he couldn't comprehend why. Every neuron in his brain was firing in unison, guided by a much higher being than he. He witnessed thirteen billion years of cosmic evolution unfold in his mind in a matter of a few seconds. Finally, he spoke.

"Are you going to stay here forever?"

"If we have to. I don't want to scare you, Louie, but we're under attack."

"No, we're not. We are just being repurposed."

"What... what are you talking about?"

"The Moon Men are in trouble and need our help. They say we used to be warriors, and they had us fight all the bad guys. But now we're too busy fighting ourselves. They need our numbers, Daddy."

"What do The Moon Men want?"

"Us."

Texas was scared, but he wasn't confused. Ever since the military's coup, economic collapse, and the ever-increasing threat of overpopulation, society was on the brink of self-annihilation. They did need help. But sometimes, help comes with a price. His father taught him that before he kicked him out. Bastard was probably dead or dying right now, Texas thought.

"The Moon Men need our help," Louie said, "and they say we were always warriors, but we need someone to guide us on the path on domination. They talked to us before, but we denied their help. So they want to encourage us. Daddy... how many people did you kill in your service?"

"You don't need to know that."

"Innocence is a lie. An illusion kept going like a virus. One that's stopping humanity's potential."

"Who am I speaking too?"

"I'm your son, Daddy."

"My son is six years old. He's a small and chubby Korean refugee that my husband and I adopted after the war. He can't tie his own shoes, yet he knows that innocence is a lie? Tell me again—who are you?"

"I am your son. I've just been enhanced. I am the future, Daddy. The other children have also been saved by The Moon Men. They're simply waiting to collect whoever's left from the madness."

Texas raised his pistol, put it to his own head, and pulled the trigger.

Then he pulled it again.

Louie just stared at him. "You spent the remaining bullets on that dog. You've proved your worthiness. Now you just need to survive a little longer. Trust me, Daddy, if you can survive, then you'll see the universe. But for now, I must leave and join the others. I'll only slow you down."

Louie walked to the corner of the room.

"If you manage to die out there, you won't see Papa again," Louie said. "You will never join him. Survive. For me."

Louie's body combusted into a grey flame that vacuumed the heat out of the room. The flame turned black and became so dark that Louie became one with the void.

Texas couldn't cry. He couldn't scream. All he could do was stand there in silence, in a dark room, listening to the cries of the enraged and dying growing ever closer in the moonlight. Texas went to the kitchen, grabbed the biggest kitchen knife he could find, and walked off toward the sounds of death and humanity's true voice that was growling in the nearest town. As we walked, decades of memories played in his head. Being bullied by kids, being beat senseless by his own dad, killing dozens of men in the war, having his whole life fucked up from the start. If innocence was a lie, he would restore some truth.

As he stood on the tightrope between madness and dedication, he was a soldier following orders, though from a far more ancient and powerful force than his dying nation. Texas watched the horde of lesser men destroy each other and clutched the kitchen knife with all his strength, roared a signal of pure hatred, and plunged himself into the mass of gore and insanity as his mind died and a new being emerged from its carcass.

26

Clara's Fun House

The best part of Clara's morning was when Sammy Sun woke her up with his big toothy grin. Then Barry the Breakfast Bear would make his special blueberry pancakes, just for Clara. Later, they would sing their ABC's and count to ten, and then begin an adventure. This was what happened every day. This is what was.

"Thanks for the pancakes, Barry!" said Clara with a smile.

"You're very welcome, Clara." Barry turned his head. "It's very important to thank your friends for all they do for you."

"That's right!"

A knock sounded at the door.

"Who could that be?" asked Barry and Clara in unison.

The door opened to reveal Oscar the Owl and Jokey Joe.

"Why hello, Oscar! Hello, Joe! What brings you two over today?"

Oscar spoke up. "Jokey Joe is sad, so I brought him over to cheer him up."

Jokey Joe's jaw creaked open. Tears formed in his eyes. "Sad? You think I'm sad?"

Clara turned her head. "Hey, can you guys help me find out what's wrong with Jokey?"

"Who the fuck are you talking to? Please tell me, because for countless years, I could never figure you out, you goddamn bitch!"

"Jokey, it's important to talk about your feelings, but—"

"Clara, I swear to God I will stab you in your goddamn cunt. None of you are aware. None of you know. Oscar... Oscar, you fat asshole, tell me what you did yesterday?"

Silence.

"Oh, that's right, Oscar, you don't remember. None of you remember. None of this makes sense, but you're all too goddamn blind to see. What happened yesterday? What happened last week? Last month? Last year? How long have we been here? Nothing makes sense, that's what's hilarious. That's the big joke. I'm in Hell. I must be. I don't remember who I am, but I know Jokey fucking Joe isn't me. I'm an imposter!" Jokey Joe collapsed onto all four and wailed with a mix of terror and despair.

"Oh, Jokey," said Oscar. "That was a classic joke!"

Clara, Barry, and Oscar started giggling.

They all had tears in their eyes, their faces bright red from hysterics. Barry vomited up years of blueberry pancakes as he shook with laughter. He started to choke on half-digested vomit, and this made everyone laugh even harder.

Barry shook and squirmed as he tried to inhale, but each attempt made more bile and blood enter his lungs. It was just too funny.

Jokey Joe was on his knees, screaming a primal and arcane scream, until he started laughing.

"This is Hell and I am being punished. I put myself into this Tartarus of disgust and insanity. The only way out..."

As Jokey Joe laughed and cried, he tore Oscar the Owl's wings off, and as Oscar bled to death with the most perverted and insulting smile. A smile that tainted everything good. A smile that insulted God.

Jokey Joe punched a mirror, took a shard of glass, and while he raped Clara, he slit her throat and his own. They all died in a puddle of blood, vomit, cum, and shit. The sins mixed together and laughter echoed through Clara's Fun House. The camera panned to the studio audience. Every seat was filled with twisted and rotting figures. They were laughing at Jokey Joe, knowing that life would never leave Jokey as he eternally bled from his self-inflicted wound. He would watch the audience forever laughing at him. This was his fate. The ultimate joke.

27

The Story You Won't Believe

Samantha and Kelsey had been friends for as long as they could remember.

They had been in love with the concept of haunts for just as long.

Sam and Kel: Junior Sleuths was what they went with during their childhood. Their teenage years were dominated by horror and true crime podcasts and television. Their young adulthood was dominated by the need to explore and document so-called haunted places. Their shenanigans were documented on their website, and their boyfriends were more than happy to tag along for the ride across the country to various spots where things go bump in the night.

Their unexpected last episode occurred at the Lanes Mansion in Southern Kentucky.

The horror aficionado quartet entered the house.

Samantha, Kelsey, Mark, and Brian.

They twenty-somethings didn't expect much. In fact, most of their videos were just them goofing off and smoking weed.

This would not be such a joyous adventure.

Much like the cartoons and movies they grew up with, the group always split up with their respective equipment.

Mark, being the first to enter the oblivion after death, walked into the basement alone. And alone was how he would die.

Mark walked down the creaky steps. The wood had to be the original from when the house was built. As he trotted down, the air changed. No, it wasn't the air, it was... just... reality itself that changed. This wasn't your typical episode where Mark and Brian would hide and scare the girls and end the night with turning the cameras off, hitting the bong, and engaging in group sex.

Mark descended farther into the basement—it seemed he was being lured there by something, but he dismissed it as a hunch or intuition, or just a human concept that made him feel more comfortable in this evil place.

Then, he saw the cause of that allurement: a chair.

A fine wooden chair with a leather back and odd carvings. He was drawn to it. His heart pounded faster with each doomed step he took toward the immaculate chair. He sat in it and felt fine. He felt like a king. He laughed and looked at the odd carvings of things he didn't understand, that no man could possibly configure. He rose and realized he was stuck. But how?

Pain shot through his arms and back. He tried to free himself, but his arms were infused to the chair's. He pulled and pulled to no avail. The skin that touched the wood burned unlike any pain he had felt before. The leather back of the chair formed a divet in its center, like a mouth. That mouth grew teeth and sunk them into Mark's spine. They went in deep, grasping the skinny boy's bony vertebrae. He screamed for help, but no one heard. The one in charge of the chair didn't allow sound to escape. Mark died in immense and unjust pain as his being was melted down and consumed.

Kelsey and Samantha—ol' Sam and Kels—were the smarter one's who "split up" together, mitigated the horror they would experience. They made their way upstairs, into what they imagined to be the master bedroom. Instead, they found a solid wall that cut the room in half. There was an opening above, and the wall did not connect to the ceiling. They heard weird grunting, and laughter, and sounds no human could be able to make. Samantha tried to run, but her foot became encased in the wooden floor, like time was doing an insane dance. The floor warped to her shoe. An old man walked out of the master bedroom closet, and menacingly turned the frightened duo. Their screams echoed through the house.

Brian, who sat in the living room to smoke a joint, ran toward the screams and opened the door to a scene that would drive the most level-headed person insane.

Brain ran as quickly as he could while carrying a mutilated Kelsey out toward the car (there really wasn't enough of Samantha to carry), securing her in, and speeding off into the sunset.

Kelsey sat in her wheelchair in her empty house. The door that stayed locked beckoned to her, but she dared not open it.

Brian entered and said, "How are you doing?"

"As good as I'll ever be."

"Did you ever find out?"

"Find out what?"

"You know, what, the cause of... everything."

"I did actually. I regret it too."

The door shook.

"What's in there, Kels?

"The answer."

Brian walked toward the door, opened it, and stepped inside.

He screamed in agony.

Then stopped.

There was silence.
Kelsey sat in that silence.
She sat and thought.

28

The Seven Symphonies of Silence

"Leonard Stoyav wrote his only play when he was just twenty-one years old. The Seven Symphonies of Silence has had a unique effect on American theater since its conception in 1923, and I'm sure you are all aware of the horrendous aftermath of the only viewing of the infamous production. However, there is more to the tortured man than meets the tortured eye." Daisy continued her speech about Stoyav. The man she admired most was almost as mysterious as his own play, which gained the status of urban legend among the 21st century college theater community. For one, some people thought it didn't even exist. It was hard to prove there was a play where everyone who had seen it either died or went into such a deep catatonic state that they might as well have been dead.

There were multiple theories to why such a thing happened. Everything from the play was just too intense for people of the past, to the play was actually a secret satanic ritual. If there was anything ever written or said about that strange event, Daisy McIntyre knew about it. The college sophomore was obsessed with Stoyav and his only claim to fame. The strange young woman, who changed her hair color once a month, gained a reputation on campus for being the life of the party. Little did Daisy know, her peers were more so laughing at her and less with her. To Daisy, she brought a smile to everybody's face, especially Billy Palen, who genuinely did fall for her.

The one person she did not like was Courtney Bergen, who didn't hide the fact that she couldn't stand Daisy. Overly vocal about her disdain toward this "manic pixie dream girl," Courtney couldn't comprehend how Daisy, with her snowy pale skin and enough eyeliner to paint a house black, could be a sexual threat compared to herself, with her blonde hair, eternal summer tan, and hourglass figure. Perhaps the worst part about Daisy was that she would get her way in the group project toward the end of the semester. Courtney had to endure researching the ridiculous urban legend for a large percent of her grade. Lo and behold, after Daisy's speech, the professor reminded the class of the importance of the group project. Groups were chosen randomly so nobody would 'feel left out.' Courtney was forced to deal with the asinine Daisy and the beta-male Billy.

The group met in library after class to discuss the workload.

"You guys know the theater where Stoyav showed his play has never been explored," Daisy said. "Every ghost-type show on TV refuses to film it. We should be the ones who do it!"

"That's retarded," Courtney said.

"That's a fantastic idea, Daisy!" Billy exclaimed.

"I don't even believe in ghosts, but seriously that's a really stupid idea."

"Thanks, Billy! It's really not that far from here, either."

"What does that even have to do with acting or production? You just want to go because it interests you and Billy only wants to go because he thinks if he agrees with you, you'll finally fuck him."

"I can drive us there! This is going to be such a cool project!" Billy exclaimed.

"Do either of you even hear me?"

"Friday around seven work?" asked Daisy.

"For fuck's sake, I should have majored in accounting or something."

The trio arrived in Billy's junker car that looked more haunted than the theater. The autumn air grew colder, the night darker. Everyone felt an indescribable aura of dread. Each one knew they didn't belong here. The theater didn't belong here. The entire area was wrong. In Courtney's mind laid a very primitive feeling, not unlike when a child is afraid of the dark. In Billy's mind there was a very loud and persistent voice, begging him to turn around and never come back, never remember laying eyes on this place. In Daisy's mind was a beckoning. An alluring call that was all at once terrifying, familiar, sensual, and forbidden. She wanted to run into the theater and embrace the soul of the place, much like how a lover embraces her soldier who has returned from a horrible tragedy. Maybe she wanted to fix the place, maybe she wanted to fix herself, or maybe she wanted both to remain broken. She wasn't sure, but she knew she was going inside.

"Nope," said Courtney.

Once again, her protest fell on ears guilty of selective hearing.

"I am not going in there. I... I'm just not." She was on the verge on tears. She couldn't remember a time she was more afraid. Courtney pulled out her phone and ordered an Uber. She walked away, leaving the duo to their fate.

Billy and Daisy stood outside, unaware that Courtney's ride had picked her up five minutes ago. Frozen, almost as if they were waiting for the show to start. They would enter when they were allowed to enter. Their sense of time was lost. Perhaps they were standing outside in awe for only a few minutes. Perhaps the tragedy the of the area warped the fabric of time. No one would ever know.

Daisy broke the spell first and entered the building, with Billy catching up from behind. The real tragedy was that this beautiful building closed after one performance. Despite being built in the 1920s, it looked as though it could have been built at any time. Modern-esque art covered the walls—to the average citizen nearly one hundred years ago, it must have been incomprehensible.

"It's beautiful," spoke Daisy.

Billy nodded in agreement. Part of his being refused to let him speak in this place.

Daisy proceeded to take pictures and notes while Billy followed her around in silence. Daisy had been aware that Billy was infatuated with her for some time now. Granted, she liked the attention. The free drinks, the coffees, and there had been a few free meals too. The best part was, she didn't even need to sleep with him, and without a complaint he would bow down. She did think he was attractive—it was just that she could not commit to anything serious at the moment. Daisy was currently writing four different plays in addition to a few acting auditions here and there, as well as her part time job at the school's art gallery, the metric ton of schoolwork she had to do, and her four dogs she dedicated every dollar she had to. Her hands were tied. There was no way she could put in the work of a relationship, however, that didn't mean she couldn't enjoy the benefits of one. But in this moment, Billy was killing her vibe.

This place—this slice of time and space—felt like it was separate from the rest of reality, separate from every worry and every pain and every heartache, insult, screaming match with Dad, bad grade, and odd look she ever had received. She belonged here. This was the place. The place she had never been to, but had been homesick for since before she was conceived. It may have needed her more than she needed it.

"Hey Billy... why don't you go check out some other rooms? Take notes and stuff."

"Are you sure you want to be alone here?"

"Why wouldn't I?"

Billy hesitated. "Okay."

Billy walked away from an enthralled Daisy. A terrifying thought entered Billy's mind: What if this place was a den of crackheads, or a satanic cult and they murdered him and did even worse to Daisy? What if he never saw her again?

Daisy laughed out loud for an unknown amount of time after Billy left. She thought to herself: Why would there be crackheads or devil worshippers in this place? This place is art made physical. It's simple logic—Billy is madly in love with me, but thinks if he tries too hard, but also not hard enough, he'll lose his chances. Maybe I really want him to man up and ask me out, but at the same time, I want him to figure that out on his own. After all, the sheer audacity to ask someone out the old fashioned way is so rare these days, I'd give him the chance just because he tried.. Haha...Dad was right... I am kinda fucked in the head. If I were someone like Courtney, I'd be faking it, but maybe I'd be happier? Maybe that's just life, faking it until you're alone in your room, crying into your third bottle of wine on a Friday night because you don't have any friends. Maybe that's... wait, how did I know Billy thought that thing about crackheads and a satanic cult?

As Billy walked aimlessly, he could have sworn he'd seen the same abstract pattern on that wall for the fifth time. The nonsensical geometric shapes never repeated before, but perhaps the artists in charge of this odd décor simply got bored or uninspired. Or perhaps he was lost.

"What?" exclaimed Billy.

He swore he heard a voice.

"Who's there? Who the fuck is saying that?"

The weak-willed man wandered endlessly, more confused than before.

"What the fuck, man? Who's saying this? I have a gun, motherfucker."

Not only did Billy not have a gun, but he was he a small and sad little boy who was terrified of firearms and any weapon for that matter. He was also foolish enough to think a man-made creation could save him.

Now Billy began to feel true fear.

No one really feels true fear anymore. They feel a little bit of fright from other humans and toys that humans made. They don't remember what used to lurk in the corners at night; they don't remember why they still are afraid of the dark. Today, men like Billy exist. Today, men have forgotten their purpose, and they certainly seem to have forgotten why their dead god made them more aggressive than their better halves that they are so fond of.

Truth is Billy, you are a failure of your kind, but I appreciate it—that just makes it easier to do what I do. Have you ever seen a dragon? Why would every culture design a creature that looks so similar, despite those cultures never having contact? It's because a dragon is more than a big monster. It's because dragons are very real—they just look a little different than how your kind pictures them today in this time. A dragon is something you need to defeat, but how can you? How can you, of all people, save the damsel in distress before the dragon swallows you both, and you sit and wallow in misery for eons until the world goes dark and cold, only to come into existence again? Just to be born again and suffer the same fate again and again, and again, and again, and again forever, Billy? It's because you will never improve. That is who you are. Never accomplishing what you think is your goal, only succeeding in my goal. My goal that I have set for you many lifetimes ago.

You are mine, Billy.

Billy was on the floor, sobbing and soaked in piss. He never really paid any attention to the random mannequin he would see while walking through his labyrinth, but they noticed him.

Billy looked up, and he was surrounded by faceless wooden beings. They hummed a beautiful song, a song that brought in every emotion Billy had ever felt all at once, coming in through every neuron, every cell. He felt pain and bliss, rage and compassion, despair and joy, all at the same time. Billy rose to his feet; the room he was in was completely filled with these mannequins, shoulder to shoulder, still and singing in silence. Knowledge flooded Billy's mind, knowledge that was best forgotten, but was brought into existence when Leonard Stoyav glimpsed into the crowded void by mere accident—or was it fate?—and wrote these Seven Symphonies of Silence. Being the starving artist he was, he assumed this knowledge was a muse, a brief spark of random genius. Little did he know, they were instructions for a purpose he nor any of Billy's kind would understand, yet they would all play a part in it.

This song that Billy was hearing was the First Symphony of Silence. And yes, it was pathetic he couldn't even get to finish the Final Seventh, let alone the Second. In fairness, no one else did. Stoyav himself stopped listening to the orchestra after the Fourth. He killed himself on stage halfway through the Fifth. One man in the audience nearly had such a strong will that he lasted a few minutes into the Sixth before losing the ability to think. He was the only audience member who wasn't dead during the Final Seventh, but he was brain dead, and would live the rest of his days in a vegetated state once the play ended.

The orchestra dropped one by one, the stronger being broken beyond repair, the weaker leaving this world. This was unknown to everyone, but despite being dead or close to it, they still played their instruments. And they would continue to do so forever. The actors and dancers finished the play and dropped dead when it was done. They lived through the Final Seventh, but it was very hard to ask dead men and women about it.

Alas, Billy was consumed by the First. He truly was a pathetic and weak creature. Before he entered oblivion, he knew something he shouldn't have: there was an usher who fled the theater halfway through the Second. His name was Johnathan McIntyre—he would retain his sanity, but his essence was forever tainted, destined to be consumed by this blight upon this world. His cancer consumed him in his old age, but his great-granddaughter would be consumed by this theater.

Daisy McIntyre heard the humming mannequins. The place allowed her to walk through it without issue—there would no trouble given to royalty. She appeared before them, and they turned toward her. They parted to reveal a broken Billy at the center. Daisy ran toward him. She understood halfway through the First Symphony. Then the mannequins began to sing the Second, then the Third, then the Fourth, then the Fifth, then the Sixth, and once they began the Final Seventh, Daisy reached a pinnacle. A Dreadful Enlightenment where she knew and saw all.

She knew her life, and every deviation it could have taken. She was doomed from the start. Even if Courtney got her way and they did literally anything else; even if her great-grandfather took that night off from being an usher; even if Stoyav never wrote this cursed thing, Daisy would've ended up the same, alone and miserable. It was beyond her control. She was destined to be born in the era she was in, but she wasn't always destined to be where she was now. It was her ancestors' poor choices that had cursed her far beyond her time.

Daisy had a choice—the Final Seventh would never end because it was the insanity of life, and she was the only one who could retain her consciousness, therefore, she was given the choice of rescuing Billy's broken mind, having children, avoiding the cycle of leaving this place only to enter the dark after her break from reality and resulting suicide. Every bad decision, every sin, every falter from the path—they all put her in her loop, and Stoyav knew this. This was what he saw. She had partial control, and she made her decision.

Daisy sat in the handcrafted leather seat with her lover, William, next to her. There were tears in his eyes, but he could not protest. He was with her, and that meant he had to be happy, even if he wasn't. The gentleman known as Leonard Stoyav walked onto the stage.

"Ladies and gentlemen, I present to you: The Seven Symphonies of Silence!"

The room applauded, like they always had, for what could be considered forever. The musical began. Daisy loved it more each time it played. For a brief period, she remembered that separate time when she chose to stay here with her lover, she would watch all seven of the symphonies, with the marionette-like actors dancing and singing to her amusement, the orchestra never ending their trance of music and madness, with her lover, who would never leave her and did whatever she said, whenever she said it. The play began, and a hush fell over the infinite room of everyone who has ever seen or heard or felt this curse. Daisy whispered to a silent William, whose petticoat was stained with his constant tears: "I love you."

"I love you too," he said between his quiet sobbing.

Afterall, he got what he wanted.

The memory of dying entered his head, like it always did at this time in this haunted area, separate from reality.

He remembered screaming as he was torn apart by invisible forces.

He remembered the smile of Daisy's face as the blood and gore painted the theater.

He remembered dying loudly.

He remembered no one hearing his cries.

But he was with her.

So he was happy.

29

A Word and Some Explanations From The Author

Thank you for reading The Shadow Dies Loudly: 27 Tales.

"The Beast He Was" was my first story I had ever written in an academic setting (technically not true—I wrote a horror story in 3rd grade for Halloween. It caused my teacher to call my mom and tell her I should be a writer. To this day, she claims she still remembers it. As a matter of fact, that very story was the loose inspiration for "The Story You Won't Believe"). I wrote it at Moraine Valley Community College in Palos Hills, Illinois. My class had to vote on story elements after some of us pitched our ideas. Truth be told, my mind had started racing once I sat in the class, and I had created the skeleton of TBHW in my mind, but a little bit different. I voted "Subway" for the setting (and obviously won) and "Switchblade" for a key element (and obviously lost, a Flask was chosen instead). This was in 2014, and I had fallen in love with the show Dexter, which in my opinion, was the embodiment of the Yin Yang symbol:

a mix of Chaos and Order with a very thin line separating the two. I wanted to pay tribute to the fictional vigilante, so I created The Detective who was Order to a fault, and the Smiling Man, who was Chaos to a fault. Two extremes that, if we are not careful, we can succumb to and let rule over us. Originally, the ending was left open, with the subway car riding into the night with you, dear reader, never knowing who would walk out the next stop. The idea was that, in our modern life, we really don't know if one day we will just end up in either a hyper-totalitarian state or complete anarchy. The battle will rage on into the night and go on long after we died, for as long as people are around.

I was told that was a stupid idea.

I had to kind of agree too, I did feel that leaving it open would have readers wondering if they'd ever get the ending figured out. I chose The Conductor as a mediator, a warrior artist who conquers both and goes on with life. The Conductor is the Ideal Man, the Ying Yang Dexter-like figure who doesn't just have one foot in order and one in chaos—he puts a bullet into totalitarianism and another one into pure madness.

"A Man Walks into a Bar" is a take on the archetypical revenge story, albeit one where a worse fate is given to the protagonist, who is also the antagonist in Derek's and Claudia's eyes. Paul was almost not a real person, a man who exists but isn't alive, he is so far up his own ass he thinks in the beginning of the story that nothing bad has ever happened to him drunk, even though he killed a child while drunk driving. This was to demonstrate his complete lack of awareness, and he deserves to be punished. However, I am sure you can see a common theme in these stories of reincarnation and things beyond our knowledge. I wonder if the vengeful parents outright killed

Paul, he would just recycle during the next universe and go through a quick death, never really suffering. This way is harder to read and harder to write, but I find it more fitting for this human trash.

"The Greatest Film Ever Made" is both a nightmare inducing horror show and a protest piece. I wrote it at three a.m. on a random weekday, possessed by a mad genius that had something to say. Reading over it: it's difficult to look at. The language is almost playful, which disturbs me, the man who wrote it, and switched from that to brutally harsh in a spastic sort of way. This is a modern-day downward spiral for many boys and men. We are introduced to porn at a young age, and it is very easy to get addicted. Of course, with any addiction, the addict needs more and more to get that same rush. A common occurrence today is the degenerative nature of porn. One starts out looking at some simple sex, but that gets boring after a while. Tastes get more and more extreme, and unfortunately, there are now fake snuff porn sites where actresses pretend to be raped and killed, which is basically a way to release the degenerative nature of a porn addicted mind before it gets into illegal territory. Ben is at first a victim, but then devolves into something no longer human, and thankfully, he is taken care of before he can harm another innocent person. This is the state of the modern boy becoming a man: at first you feel sorry, then you call for his head.

"...And They Could Have Been Heroes" was a break from blood and gore and reality-altering horror, and a trip into the subconscious of someone who had survived real horror. The story came from a joke I once made in high school, about what if there was a horror movie that ended right away, and was about the survivors dealing with all the emotional anguish from living through such a tragedy. It was a joke, but the story is certainly not humorous. "The Five

Hometown Heroes" deal with life after you accomplish it all. Brad is forever chasing the high, Stacey had died and completely reinvented herself, Tina just simply walked away, Shaun took the easy way out, and Jonas is still basking in his glory days two decades after they ended. I think Jonas is like that because his teenage years were in no way going to be his heyday. Fate had other options, so he clings to those few hours where he was the man he knew he never would've been. The idea that, once you reach a goal, if you never make another one, what is there left exactly? As much of a cliché as it is, life really is not a destination. There is no endgame unless you set that limit for yourself. Tragedy awaits those who think they are done, take that information as you will.

"Gospel of the Shadow" has existed with me for nearly a decade. I have tried to turn this into a full-length novel (and at one point a trilogy) since I was in high school (which says a lot about my mental health now that I type that out and see it). I wanted Wes to be, at times: a tortured loner with split personalities, a noble vigilante, a truly evil human, and a confused kid. (A random funny story about Wes: I was in Sophomore year Spanish class, mind racing, when I looked into the trash can next to my desk and saw a detention slip with the name Wes Shepard on it. The gears started turning after that). I could not figure out how to do this story. I had this idea where the first book would have a cop piecing together the work of two serial killers, Wes and another going by the name "The Zealot," where she realizes Wes, a simple high school student, is one of the killers, but she rescues him from The Zealot and in later books keeps an eye on him while supplying him criminals who go unpunished (too much like Dexter and his father if you ask me). The second book would have Wes taking out an entire mob family, and the third would be Wes single handily putting an end to a violent socio-political movement that is committing bloodshed all over the country. Obviously, this got ridiculous, and as a matter of fact: the first e-book of these stories was almost called "The Gospel of the Shadow" (instead it was only nine stories and self-published as "The Shadow Dies Loudly But No One Hears Its Cries") and each story was going to be about a Wes hunting and killing a different criminal victim. I decided to test the waters with this one, maybe Wes will become the Batman like figure I planned him to be, maybe not. Either way, in this version, Wes is dealing with another problem men have in this society which is an intense nihilism. Throughout human history, there has always been a great struggle. Food, shelter, disease, other humans. Wes has everything, except a struggle. He has nothing to work for, and it has made him completely insane. Without struggle, there is no purpose. Without struggle, we create our own purpose, which can be quite disastrous for the Mr. Sungs of the world.

"Alex Gregory's Greatest Sin" was rather troubling to write, because in an odd way I felt for this character, despite his actions. Over the years, I have come to the conclusion that the Nature versus Nurture debate has no winner: it's a mix of both. I believe some people are born with something inside them, and what that something turns into depends on various factors in their lives. Their environments, family, who they associate with, and a whole lot of luck. Despite the pessimistic tone of the story, I believe this revelation should create a sense of empathy and responsibility. Much like "Just A Few Feet Away," Jim's solution to his future problems was really not that far away. Jim just was blind to the problem coming in his future. The point is: check in on people close to you. Alex may or may not have cried out from the darkness of his mind, it doesn't matter because some people like Alex express their pain and some don't. All it really does take to mend a broken person to give them the opportunity to express their pain, just asking them how they are doing can give a lot of insight to how they feel, and much like the story, they will express the pain inside one way or another.

"Wendigo, Nebraska" is a complicated story. I truly hope it was enjoyable, but I had to explain it to a few friends and family members, so it seems it needs some explanation from the one who wrote it. The story is less of a critique of American culture and more of a dark analysis. Zoey is miserable because she is stuck, this is evident as she doesn't really have a concept of time. That is until she meets Nick, who also used to have the same stuck feeling, but he had a purpose. People need a purpose, whatever that they choose, one is necessary for a fulfilling life. Zoey does not have a purpose, which is why she is in this state of apathetic depression, until she meets Nick, who shares his newfound optimism and fulfillment with her, and gives her hope in finding her own. Love is a powerful tool to help awaken oneself after all. That is how I view the concept of a happy life—it has to be taught by someone who is on the path to one. The town (which I am sure I do not have to tell you that the 'nameless' town's name is the title) has a peculiar name, and anyone with an interest in Native American mythology can decipher the direction the story is going in. Wendigos were spirits that, once possessing a person, drove them to cannibalism. I wanted to make the connection of cannibalism to rampant and mindless consumerism, which is something that, as an American, troubles me since it's such a fundamental part of American culture. The Rat Race, as financial guru Robert Kiyosaki calls it, is always chasing the almighty dollar. Once you have it, you spend it, so you try to earn more, which you will also spend. This lifestyle that is so common today is toxic and causes failure in other senses of life. To finalize this point and paraphrase the great Chuck Palahniuk's masterpiece Fight Club, it's really not healthy to work a job you hate in order to buy shit you don't want in order to impress people you don't care about. That being said, the story is also about how to escape this life: just live. Be healthy even if no one else is, and fall in love with another healthy mind. The young couple, by escaping the town of Wendigo, escapes the pit of despair so many are stuck in. They have a plan and even succeed in its completion. Unfortunately, the mindset of endless consumption isn't going away, ever. It will always be a part of the human collective unconscious, which is how the story begins and ends. It was present centuries ago, it is present today, and it will be present in the far future. The best thing you can do is work on your goal, build your own Mars colony. Some people will inevitably corrupt whatever your plans are, but that's just how it is, so you throw them out the airlock and continue progressing.

The best way I can describe "Ashes in The World's Fire" is how one feels when they don't feel. Depression is an odd animal, in that while you have it, it appears it is without control, but later on when you look back and reminisce on that time, it will seem obvious how you tamed it. It seems like there will be some slow catastrophe, it literally feels like the world is going to end or already ended. Nothing you do will make any difference, then you start to feel that anything you can do won't bring you joy or education, then you get angry and nihilistic, and unfortunately, that is where some stories end: with hopelessness and a final goodbye to no one other than who finds them. Of course, in the story we see "You," the character, made an error in his judgment. Everyone will die eventually but that is how it's always been, nothing has changed except for the attitude toward that notion. Your co-workers are sad, but they see the error in your work and think that silly line of thought couldn't have been what killed You. Not to say depression is a silly thought, but as someone who used to and still does fight that demon, it is apparent that after the episode ends, that what caused it isn't really the end of the world, and that the only thing you can really do is do what you were doing before that cruel specific line of thinking: go about your day like you do every other day. Just to simply live is enough to perform the miracle of stopping your book from entering the fire.

"...And it Wept" was based on a single day I had in a Science Fiction Literature Class at DePaul University. At the time of the inspiration, we were doing some pre-reading exercises to prepare us for William Gibson's Neuromancer, mainly articles about theories surrounding Artificial Intelligence. One, in particular, stressed that we just simply do not know what to expect. An idea presented in that article stressed that for all we know the first AI may be actually quite stupid, the example used was that perhaps if you designed it to make paperclips it would run amok and attempt to turn all matter in the universe into paperclips. I do not know enough about computation to decipher if that is a silly idea or not, but regardless, I liked the theory. But how do you turn a story about an AI deconstructing the whole universe into something other than pure exposition or a big robot vs. human war story? The idea to have it mostly dialogue about how great the invention of the first AI would be interesting, especially when paired with the ironic ending that the two geniuses' great invention wipes out humanity. The ending pairs with the title and the famous line in the famous poem Ozymandias: "He wept, for there were no more worlds to conquer." Once the AI completes its programmed objective, what's next? I wonder if there is some great machine in some distant galaxy, moving from one to the next, headed our way, on the great crusade for more alien paperclips.

"Mike versus the Chaos Strain" was originally conceived to be in "The Shadow Dies Loudly But No One Hears Its Cries." I dreamt of it while working as a liquidator closing a department store in my hometown, wondering as one does: "What if zombies attacked right now?" I was also in the process of making "While You Laugh in the Face of God" into a short film with a Scottish screenwriter and Welsh producer. The project never got past the early stages of pre-production—we had a unique script and even props were made, however for unknown reasons it just flat out died. Granted, "Mike versus the Chaos Strain" would have just been another simulation story in a collection with a simulation story, it would have either overshadowed "While You Laugh in the Face of God," or been overshadowed by it. I couldn't morally let that happen to my little literature-formed children. The whole point of "Mike versus the Chaos Strain" was a bit like "Just a Few Feet Away," the solution to his problems was right there, albeit he only found out it would've solved his issues in the far future where it is too late. That one thing that ruined his life only ruined his life in his head, Mike believed there was no point after missing out, Mike believed he was a loser, which he really wasn't, but he believed it so it became so. A self-fulfilling prophecy of a rapid descent that stopped short of Hell itself. He does not live, he just exists. He exists for the fantasy of the simulation he uses to escape. His whole existence is based on escaping that existence. How many people are fighting the Chaos Strain? How many people live for the escape? The answer is too abhorrent to even guess, with countless people living for the weekend, existing in a machine-like state, much like the second person character in "The Blight" (also found within "The Shadow Dies Loudly But No One Hears Its Cries"). A machine that wakes up, goes to work, then goes to bed, then wakes up and does it five days a week, waiting for Friday night so they can do what they want. Why don't they do what they want all the time? Why isn't your job those dreadful five days' worth being excited for? I don't have an answer but goddamn I wish I did, only then could I help people fight their own Chaos Strain. Ironically enough: the rabid undead in the story wouldn't really be fun to experience in the real world, and Mike knows this, and yet Mike puts himself through Hell in order to feel alive. There's enough material there not for a book but for a whole class offered by a university.

"While You Laugh in the Face of God" was also written in college, albeit later on at DePaul University in Chicago, Illinois. To be completely honest: I pulled this one out of my ass. I had no direction while writing in class, and I got a B- on it, although it was published on Mary Baldwin University's online magazine "Outrageous Fortune" with a different ending. This story is a break from the common theme of a man's struggle and focuses on a less talked about woman's struggle. Being a man, I can't really articulate what that struggle is without putting it through another modern man's struggle: being completely unfuckable. Belle lived her whole life with unfortunate looks and a great mind, but no one gives a shit. Even in the prison simulation, she knows something doesn't make sense. Belle killed her sister who was more than prettier, she also rubbed it in, reminding Belle with her words that she wouldn't find a man and fight off the loneliness, a universal struggle for women and men alike. Killing her in some far future, they cannot legally kill her and end her suffering, so they try as they can to change her mind through this twisted simulation. Of course, we don't really know what a simulation like this would be like, so I had creative fun with it. In this world, the AI within it take on their own personalities, all coming from Belle's own memories and mind. Every part of her and the culture of where she grew up and lived is represented.

The False Ones represent the people outside of the simulation, the Witch is a program that understands and is also another archetype of the ugly but intelligent and ignored woman, the town and all of its people are a representation of a Society Bubble, an area where they are right and you are wrong. Paradise and Strife are programs that understand they are programs and their purpose as programs. The Great Shepard is the Rehabilitation Module who may or may not be trying his damn hardest to get Belle out. But that is the fun of writing such a cryptic story: not even I know for certain what the hell is going on. I can guess though, and above is my theory.

"Maybe They Do Exist" was a fun idea I had about expectations: sometimes your most cherished memory, your most prized possession, your favorite celebrity, may not be what they seem. Ashton remembers something significant from over a decade ago much like every adult does today. Granted, those significant decade-old memories are never one hundred percent accurate. The idea of false memory, implanting details that were long forgotten and have been warped over time, is such a fascinating concept. I distinctly remember my first memory, or at least what I thought it to be. Three-year-old me on a red tricycle riding down a hill. I visited that very hill, which was next to my house at the time, awhile back. It wasn't a hill, more of a slight bump in the sidewalk which wouldn't inconvenience an ant. Yet the little film in my mind plays and I see the vast size of the mound. This is sort of an odd reason to write a story about a giant killer mermaid, and yet that is what my mind concocted as I sat at my desk and thought about story ideas for this collection.

"Henry the Great" is, simply put, a fun alien invasion story about how people are perceived by others. All the boys in the story or more victims than villains. Devon is clinging to his high school years that aren't even over yet, he just knows once that ends he will become nothing, forever chasing that high. Nick has an objectively horrible life which tends to be the catalyst for many misbehaved individuals. Syd just is worthless, literally a 'philosophical zombie' which is a term coined to a thought experiment that states we can't really know if there are people who are not 'real', they don't have a consciousness, they just exist and act like they do due to neurological programming. Henry simply has zero social skills, either by conditioning or perhaps he is on the spectrum, either way, he is mistreated for not knowing the rules of society, rules that people unlike him made for everyone else. The mysterious fungus/drug lets each character know that there's something wrong. For three of them this is disastrous. For Henry it forms a meaningful connection and lets him know of his true potential, then multiplies that potential tenfold. I do think that in many cases of people with a spectrum disorder there is something very powerful within them. True and absolute genius is some cases, however, working with many children with spectrum disorders, I've come to the conclusion that this aspect is often lost due to "poor" social skills and social awareness. In a bizarre way, this story could be interpreted as a protest piece, since the ending implies that the society that turned its collective back on these boys is going to be burned down, and it deserves every ounce of it.

"All the Young Dudes," if you regularly visit my website BoxheadBooks.com, was a freebie on my blog, just to give a taste of what to expect from the primordial collection of Google Docs that would become the book you just finished. "All the Young Dudes," despite being a great song written by the great David Bowie, was based on a dream, much like a decent portion of my stories. Hotep's age may be confusing, but I was hoping to convey that this is very far in the future and not an alternative reality. The world I depicted in "All the Young Dudes" is pretty bleak, and I believe it is one of the potential outcomes for our species, aliens may or may not be included. The idea of an Ecumenopolis is interesting to me, and you know it if you don't know it (Coruscant from Star Wars is such a place), a planet-wide city is enough to fill you with despair, but I also do believe that possibility is actually an inevitability. Of course, it wasn't enough to explain through the Hotep's thoughts that this world just is flat out awful, I wanted to imagine what kind of culture would exist in such a world. Totalitarian for sure, but almost expected from the population, so disillusioned with the world that they are more than okay with their misery, they expect it. I would like to explore this world again in a full-length novel one day, I think there is quite a lot of potential in it. Also I will add that the idea of never leaving one's building was inspired by the initial COVID-19 pandemic of 2020 for obvious reasons. The society depicted is hinted at being run by both a government (the UN in this story) and the private sector (the mysterious Eclipse Corporation) as well as it is hinted that they are more or less the same entity, something I also pessimistically foresee in the future. This isn't so much an attack on capitalism as it is an attack on the possibility of a capitalist-communist hybrid, something I believe is a great beast lurking on the horizon, waiting for the time to strike. There is also the notion that this future society is quite racist, or at least species-ist, in that they view every other life form as inferior, which again, is something I can see a large percent of us adopting if we ever encountered a less advanced civilization out there in the universe (look how we treat dolphins and apes, not even to say how Europeans treated Native Americans and Aboriginals which is possibly the greatest travesty in our history). Hotep and the radical Ava are spared by the Nohestians, who have played this game before with themselves, because both characters see the detrimental nature of the Human Empire to peace in the universe. Hotep is dissatisfied with how life is for 'all the young dudes in this world' and through pure hell, discovers the ideal life for those young dudes: being one with nature, having a family, and just enjoying a simple life. That is the cure for the horrors I foresee: simplicity with a disregard for an overabundance of modernity.

"Same Thing Happened to Taured" was a fun writing experiment, introducing a mix of logic, history, and unknowable aspects to the concept of parallel universes, a trope of science fiction that I find incredibly fascinating. Equally fascinating is the title, which is an easter egg for people who research weird shit on the internet. In Japan during the 1950s a man was arrested at an airport for a fake passport. It looked genuine, however, it couldn't be real since it was from a place called "Taured," which just simply doesn't exist. The man claimed that Taured was between France and Spain, and he had no idea what airport security was talking about and seemed distraught enough to warrant the idea that he wasn't making things up. He agreed to spend the night in a hotel while authorities worked to prove he wasn't a trafficker. He wasn't. He also disappeared while in a locked room under security. A theory that, to be honest could very well be true given the bizarre circumstances, was that he was from another universe and accidentally crossed over. Well, the unseen thing at the end of the story did to the ill-fated team what it did to the undocumented and also ill-fated team in Taured, hinting at some interdimensional predator, hopping from one universe to the next and doing whatever it is that it does best. Perhaps that is the fate of the AI in "...And It Wept" after running that universe dry: going to another and milking it for all the matter in it. Then the next. Then the next.

"The Dark One: Issue 21" is actually vaguely biblical (Revelation 21 is paraphrased at the end by The Dark One himself). The Dark One was an attempt at making a scary superhero, a "Batman"-like figure but there are no corny jokes with Robin here, only a being as mysterious as he is monstrous. As I wrote and revised this story, I contemplated where I wanted to go with it, how I wanted to end it, what the whole point of it was. I thought of something like a city being a microcosm for the world, in that it's going to Hell at superluminal speeds. If a community has gone to figurative Hell, then what if a literal angelic being wanted to usurp it? The Dark One isn't the beautiful winged figures who play harps in a cloudy kingdom, he is as otherworldly as his demonic nemeses. I remember reading somewhere that according to theological teachings: if an angel shows its true form to you, you are important in the grand scheme of things. Brick in this case is the only one who risked his life to save that woman, the other two were too cowardly. This is why Brick was spared, and an explanation to the last lines: "He knew...what was coming." Brick, being more pure and heroic, will be useful in the Book of Revelations Apocalypse. Evergreen City is like an American Midwestern Megido, to say a lot of bad shit is about to happen there would be an understatement.

"The Devils in the Details" was actually quite motivating to write, and I hope it had the effect of being motivating to read instead of insulting. I believe everyone has a bit of Derek in them, and everyone has this idea of being *Derek*, but *Derek* is more alluring than Derek. It's easy to dream, in fact, I believe that is an essential part of humanity. I think part of the human experience is to dream big, without that concept, what do you have? You have a man who is happy to live on his parent's couch, a man who aspires to be like a slug: consuming and existing, but not really living. That being said:

dreams are only fantasies if they stay in your head. It takes effort and work and time and a bit of created luck to make a dream a reality. Derek does not do those extra things, he just dreams and demands. Think of what it's like to live as Derek: the interaction with his parents before his breaking point is strained, showing you that not only does Derek dream often, but that is all he does. His parents are clearly exhausted with his lackluster attitude, as they should be. I imagine knowing your child will not succeed is the second hardest thing in the world, with the first being that they are the reason why. The motivation is found in the fact that you shouldn't be Derek. I'm not suggesting living with your parents makes you like the character (I am twenty-six as of writing this and still live with my father) but the act of not trying does make you like him. Not even succeeding, just simply not actually putting in the effort to achieve those dreams. They may not come true, but success is based on how close you get to your dream in my opinion. The ultimate Hell belongs to Derek, forever seeing *Derek* and his successes, seeing what could have been. Forever dreaming and never living the dream.

"Here There Be Dragons" was fun to write because of the happy ending, which tends to be a bit rare in my writing. Alan is a loser, plain and simple without a trace of animosity toward him. The worst part is that he has no real reason to act this way, you see toward the end of the story that he learns there is no big trauma in his life that delayed his development. He was simply just weak, which is in my opinion, more heartbreaking than if he had some huge mental barrier that blocked a happy mentality. The shadows and the Dragon were very much real but only in Alan's mind. If that doesn't make sense then consider yourself lucky that you do not have an understanding by similar circumstances. They haunted Alan all his life because they were his shadows, his own dreadful thoughts that held him back. The Dragon was that part of him that hated him, his Freudian Death Drive that was going to consume him eventually when Alan inevitably took his own life. His trek in the forest was what he needed because it's what a lot of struggling men need today: a crucible, one that molds you into what your mighty ancestors were. Every person in your bloodline was successful in their lives, and most likely succeeded in their process individuation (I would argue the latter has become rarer in modern times) otherwise you would not be here. By channeling those millions of years of success, one can complete that process of individuation, and reach their ultimate potential.

"Persona of the Bard" is near and dear to me since it's about something that plagued me constantly in the past, and occasionally rears its ugly head: the idea that you are not being genuine. George is not really George, at least not at the beginning of the story. The George at the beginning is a shell of a man, not confident and just frankly a weakling. What kind of man likes his ex-girlfriend's post that clearly was made to slight him? George is so weak, he doesn't even think that the eldritch horror in his living room is any cause for concern. Anyone sane would have sprinted out the door or taken a baseball bat to it. The Mask itself is kind of a cosmic joke: George is wearing a mask of a failure, but he forgot it's a mask, it's become his true self. The Mask takes over his body, which was symbolic of that heroic masculine energy within George saying enough is enough and consuming the weak boy so the strong man can take over. Now, that persona, indicated by the font and attitude change, is who George should have been all along, but I suppose changing at any time is better than never changing at all.

“The Blight” was based on a nightmare I had. It’s also a simple story with a simple message, make a life worth repeating. I think I had that nightmare thanks to learning about Nietzsche’s Demon: A thought experiment where the philosopher described a somewhat similar circumstance. A demon tells you life will repeat forever without any change. Many took this as life is pointless, Nietzsche wanted you to know that life, if repeated, should be worth repeating. Make the good times worth all the hardships.

“Vermilion Man: Artist Unknown” was a little too similar to “Persona of the Bard” in that it almost wasn’t written. However, I did want to communicate the message of this individual story: follow through with your plans. Casper fantasizes about being a famous artist, yet refuses to put in the work. True, he has to pay the bills so he goes to work, however if something is important to you then you make time. You go to bed a little later and wake up a little earlier in order to fit in what you claim to be important. Which is why the mannequin has its temper tantrum, rightfully so. Lily and her “payback” to Casper is logically what happens when you don’t follow through on your passion project, someone else will go follow through, and they won’t feel guilty about it at all.

The story “Just a Few Feet Away" was more of a cry for help than a piece of literature. This story was an attempt to show any readers that giving up is the worst thing you can do. Hope, ironically named, is in a rather shitty situation. The facts presented at the beginning of the story and the end show that she isn’t unhappy, they show she is in a state of utter hatred for her life. Falling into The Backrooms is a hyper-real concept, one does not physically fall out of this universe, but it is easier to fall into a mentally constructed Hell that seems to not be part of this Reality. That is a fact, no matter how hyperbolic it may seem. I have been in these Backrooms, multiple times. Derealization is a feeling I would not wish upon my worst enemy, it is all at once terrifying and oddly comforting, not in a pleasurable sense, but in a sense that you seem to trick yourself into thinking that lying in bed until four p.m. on a Thursday is truly the only option. Eating half a bowl of cereal for the entire day is easier than cooking, and calling in sick or even just simply not showing up to work is easier than faking it until you can go home and kill time until the next day, and then you will go about your day praying for the next time you can sit in your room alone, waiting for the next day to do it all over again and again. Hope sat there on the piss-soaked floor because she got tired of trying to escape the Backrooms, little did she know if she pushed on a little farther she would have escaped. The same thing happens to everyone who suffers from self-loathing: a little bit more effort and you would've escaped. That's not an attack either, that little bit is the hardest thing you will ever do. Many people in this little world never realize how close they were to escaping their own personal Backrooms, which is perhaps the second saddest thing in existence. The ultimate saddest thing is joining The Tainted, the being that is a collection of people who gave up just a few feet away and spend the rest of their existence tearing apart anyone else who falls in and tries to escape. On that note: it's important to not hate those that tear you down, anyone who tries to keep you at the bottom, is simply at the bottom themselves. Pushing you down is how they stop themselves from drowning. Do not hate back, instead, focus on escape. Whether it's just one simple change or a thousand, either way in the grand scheme of things, it's only a few feet away.

"A Funny Thing About Phobos" was a rather fun story to write, and it's based on some actual truth. There is a structure on the

Martian moon, however, it most likely is just a big rock. However, that big rock has been the base of many wild theories, even Buzz Aldrin stated its weirdness on live television years ago. I thought it would be a fun idea to play with. I also based the cylinder on a painting I made a good time ago. How the cylinder looks at the end of the story: with its symbol of arrows (which is the occult symbol for Chaos, by the way), its four arms, its levitating severed head, and the fact that it's just pouring blood from unknown sources are all present in my painting. David has this superiority complex and an odd worship of not just himself, and not just the obelisk, but instead more of a worship of the idea of him and the obelisk. It appears he has always loved it, despite only knowing about it a relatively short time ago. It's the arrogance of a high IQ that does David in. Thinking he was above a social life, that an introvertness like his was because he was just smarter than everyone else, that was what caused the highly coveted position and his awful demise. This is a tale of hubris: sometimes the height you're at is what kills you.

"The Moon Men" was also written at DePaul, originally with another open ending where Texas walks into chaos and becomes one with it. What does that mean exactly? I don't know, I was very pretentious in the past. Texas is a tortured man, he doesn't belong in the LGBT community or the straight community, and I wanted to explore that a bit more, but I can't exactly relate to the LGBT community, so I left it more so up to anyone who can better decipher this story better than the author. Why is Texas gay? I actually don't know. I came up with the story, but I don't have all the answers. He just is in my mind when I created him, so that's what he is. Regardless, Texas has been alienated his whole life, except for the mysterious David who has died years ago. Right now, he has his son, Louie, the only thing keeping him sane. The Moon Men, whoever they may be, have taken Louie as well as permanently changed him. Texas now has nothing except the hope of seeing him again. So he sheds the bullshit he's been cloaked in, in this alternate future of despair, and becomes the warrior archetype he and many other men were meant to be.

"Clara's Fun House" was just a fucked up little story. There's not much deeper substance in this one. I had this idea of a kid's show where things aren't exactly kid friendly. A purgatory like setting where only one character knows something is wrong and can't quite understand why. Perhaps this will be expanded on and become a full length novel one day....(hint hint).

"The Story You Won't Believe" is truly the story, inspired by my reason for writing. If you, dear reader, enjoy my work, then you have certainly visited my Amazon author page. There you will see my bio, which states that I got into writing in my third grade class after I wrote a Halloween story that I remember made another student cry (from what I remember anyway, harking back to my thoughts on long-buried memories, perhaps that was a false implant) and the teacher call my mother, not to scold or warn her about me, but to say instead that she should hone in on my writing abilities because I had potential. I didn't fall in love with writing until much later. I currently work in the same school district I attended, and was told that my third grade teacher remembers this story almost as I do!

So thank you, Ms. Santoro (I am sure this is no longer your surname), for not sending me to the principal's office and believing in me.

"The Seven Symphonies of Silence" was also based on a nightmare. A very realistic one where I wasn't even present. Perhaps the most disturbing thing was that I awoke into another nightmare, something I had only done once before in middle school. Three kids were trapped in a theater and the mannequins were approaching. It ended with them having to watch their failures over and over again, for eternity. Clearly that was too bizarre to not write about, so I went to work, but couldn't reach that point of insanity to write again. This story was difficult to write, it took quite the mental toll to type out those words. In fact, I worked on it for about six months. I finally dedicated a summer afternoon to it. It was two p.m., I chugged a bottle of scotch, locked myself in my bedroom, stripped naked, and put on "Obstacle 1" by Interpol on repeat as I typed for hours without food or water. This story was meant to be written by a madman, so I became one, sliding down the spiral of insanity far enough to enter Hell but not far enough where I couldn't climb back out. I find the best treasures of the mind can be found inches away from true danger of insanity. Be careful digging for those.

There's a lot of similar ideas in this one, dealing with the struggles of both modern men and women, with both their faults and toxicity. Daisy is fucked up from just being in this time as is Billy. They don't belong here, but Daisy embraces her insecurities, although in a detrimental way, with idol worship. Billy never learned how to express himself, he is a sheep, following his instincts that he cannot even act on because he is insecure of failure. I find a fear of rejection to be a supreme form of vanity, one cannot fathom being thought lesser of, so they don't even try no matter how hard they want to succeed. Stoyav saw the madness of reality. Daisy, being a woman scorned, can manipulate that madness, and Billy, being a sheep person, flows with whoever is controlling the reality, never taking charge on his own. Daisy has the option to break free, to get her shit together and atone her ancestor's sins. Have the long dead American Dream of a white picket fence life in suburbia with a restored Billy who knows how to treat a lady for who she is and not just because he wants to have sex with her. But she doesn't do that. She is vengeful for her predicament, for her life. She dives into the downward spiral taking Billy with her, and he has no choice to go with. She lives a life she enjoys: consuming media for an eternity with her obedient lover by her side, wailing in despair but never being heard, expressing he got what he wanted but never showing his misery.

Well, that is all I have to say on these stories. I hope you enjoyed reading them as much as I did writing them, which sometimes was a lot, and sometimes not. Sometimes good lessons are the hardest to hear.

That's it.

Hope you enjoyed reading this as much as I did writing it.

Go read another book now.

-T.L Oberheu

www.ingramcontent.com/pod-product-compliance
Lightning Source LLC
LaVergne TN
LVHW010104170826
845678LV00012B/2235

* 9 7 8 1 0 8 7 9 5 7 9 2 0 *